I'M HOME!
BAN (DUN)
TAB-LET? CHECK!
BABAN (DUDUN)
SNACKS AND DRINKS? CHECK AND CHECK!!
I'M GONNA GET MY GOLDEN WEEK SOLO-CAMPING PLANS...
WAKI
わき
WAKI (CLUTCH)
わき
...ALL WRAPPED UP TODAY!!
FIRST IS TO DECIDE WHERE I'M GOING...

I SAW ON A RECENT INFORMATIONAL SHOW...
...THAT THEY HAVE A BUNCH OF VINTAGE TRAINS IN GUNMA.
IT LOOKS LIKE THEY HAVE A MUSEUM THERE.
AHA!
17:01
YOKOKAWA RAIL MUSEUM
THAT'S RIGHT!
THAT MUSEUM MY SISTER WAS TALKING ABOUT!
OKAY!
LET'S GO TO THE EXHIBIT IN GUNMA FOR GOLDEN WEEK!
THEN, I JUST NEED TO FIND...
むしゃ
MUSHA (MUNCH)
むしゃ
MUSHA
...SOME OFF-THE-BEATEN-PATH CAMPSITE THAT WON'T BE TOO CROWDED.
TODAY'S GONNA BE BUSY.

16
Afro
LAID BACK CAMP
山梨530
に 11-223

16

LAID-BACK CAMP

contents

CHAPTER 88
FAREWELL, SHIMARIN'S BUN,
UNTIL SHE GROWS HER HAIR OUT AGAIN

AWW! YOU'RE REALLY GONNA CUT IT OFFFF!?
ZUUUUN (SUUUULK)
YOU DID IT BEFORE.
SO I'M COUNTING ON YOU TO CHOP IT OFF.
NNH.
NOW WHAT AM I GONNA DO FOR FUN AT SCHOOL ...?
HAAH ...
WHEN I CLOSE MY EYES, I CAN STILL SEE...
...ALL THE WORKS OF ART I MADE WITH YOUR HAIR.
THE ONE THAT REALLY WENT VIRAL ON SOCIAL MEDIA WAS THE "NEBUTA FESTIVAL" ...
WHEN WAS THIS!? WHEN DID YOU DO THIS!?
AND YOU PUT IT ONLINE !?
121
53211
57035

MY POOR FOLLOWERS.
I'LL HAVE TO TELL THEM, "I'M SO SORRY, I MUST RESIGN FROM MAKING HAIR ART."
YOU HAVE QUITE A LOT OF FOLLOWERS.
YOU MADE ALL OF THESE?
YOU'RE REALLY GOOD, SAITOU-SENPAI.
EMA-CHAN, YOUR HAIR ISN'T AS LONG AS RIN'S...
...BUT YOUR HAIR TYPE SEEMS PRETTY EASY TO PLAY WITH.
AH!
I'M COUNTING ON YOU FROM NOW ON, EMA-CHAN!
F-FOR WHAT?
HER NEW ~~TOY~~ HAIR MODEL.

NOW, MISS, HOW SHORT WOULD YOU LIKE IT?
OH, A LITTLE SHORTER. ABOUT THIS LONG.
AWW, THAT SHORT!?
EH?
IF I TRY IT ONCE, I'LL KNOW.
WHERE IS THIS PHOTO FROM, IBIKAWA-SAN?
OH, THAT PHOTO?
IT'S FROM WHEN WE WENT TO LAKE NOZORI LAST YEAR.
LAKE NOZORI?

IT'S A LAKE AT THE EDGE OF GUNMA. EVER HEARD OF IT?
HMM... NO, I HAVEN'T.
WHAT?
ISN'T LAKE NOZORI IN NAGANO?
THAT'S LAKE NOJIRI.
ISN'T IT NEAR TOGAKUSHI?
THE SCENERY SUR-ROUNDING THE LAKE MAKES IT FEEL LIKE YOU'RE IN A TOTALLY DIFFERENT COUNTRY.
IT'S A LAKESIDE CAMPSITE, BUT IT'S KINDA OFF THE BEATEN PATH.
YOU CAN SEE THE LAKE FROM THE TENT SITES. IT'S SUBLIME.
THE BUNGA-LOWS ARE PRETTY NICE AND CONVE-NIENT TOO.
OOH.

THOUGH, THE BUS THAT GOES TO THE LAKE ONLY COMES SO MANY TIMES IN A DAY.
THERE ARE HARDLY ANY SHOPS OR RESTAU-RANTS AROUND.
AND THE ROAD IS CLOSED IN THE WINTER, SO IT CAN BE DIFFICULT TO GET THERE.
BUT THE FACT THAT IT'S SO HARD TO REACH IS WHAT MAKES IT SUCH A HIDDEN GEM.
WHICH REMINDS ME, EMA-CHAN, YOU STILL HAVEN'T BEEN CAMPING YET, RIGHT?
NO. MY PARENTS AND I ARE INDOOR PEOPLE.
WHEN-EVER YOU WANT TO GO, LET ME KNOW.
I'LL LEND YOU MY CAMP-ING GEAR.
TH-THANK YOU VERY MUCH.
YEAH, SAME HERE!

I CAN LEND YOU ANYTHING YOU NEED OUTSIDE OF A TABLE AND CHAIR.
WHY NOT A TABLE AND CHAIR?
AHH, WELL...
IF YOU USE THEM OUTSIDE, THE BOT-TOMS OF THE LEGS GET ALL...
...MESSED UP ON ROCKS AND STUFF, RIGHT?
SO THAT'S DEFINITELY OUT.
I GET YOUR CONCERN, BUT THEY'RE BUILT FOR OUTDOOR USE.
LAKE NOZORI IN THE MOUN-TAINS OF GUNMA, EH...?
I WANNA SEE THIS IN PERSON SOME-DAY.

ENJOYING THE LAKE AND TAKING MY TIME ... ... WOULD BE HARD WITHOUT STAYING OVER.
GUESS I CAN'T AVOID GOING CAMPING.
OKAY, HOW ABOUT THIS?
THANK YOU. I FEEL SO MUCH LIGHTER, SAITOU.
IT'S PRETTY SHORT NOW.
I CAN'T REMEMBER THE LAST TIME MY HAIR WAS THIS SHORT.

... UH...
CHIKUWA LOOKS LIKE AN AFGHAN HOUND NOW.
THE HAIR CUT OFF OF RIN
WOW, THIS LATE AL-READY?
17:46
APRIL 27TH (MONDAY)
LATER, SAITOU, I GOTTA BE GOING...
HELLO!
HUH!?
WH-WHAT DID YOU DO?
DID YOU NOT JUST CUT MY HAIR!?
HEH! HEH! HEH! HEH! HEH! HEH!

THERE CAN BE NO RIN WITH-OUT HER BUN...
THERE'S NO GOING BACK ON THE IMAGE THE PUBLIC HAS OF YOU.
SHIMA RIN
THAT IMAGE IS ALREADY IMPRINTED UPON THE HEARTS AND MINDS OF THE MASSES.
SO...
...YOU WOULD BREAK HEARTS IF YOU GAVE UP THE BUN.
BUUUUUN!
WHY DID YOU GET RID OF IT?
who are you?
I THINK A WHOLE LOTTA FOLKS...
...WON'T EVEN RECOGNIZE YOU ANY-MORE.
NONE OF THAT WILL HAPPEN.
IN ORDER TO PREVENT SUCH A TRAGEDY...
999 YEN LIMITED TIME OFFER!!
NAMAZON
...I BOUGHT A BUN EXTENSION OFF OF NAMAZON!
BAN (BOM)
EVEN IF YOUR NATURAL BUN MUST BE LOST...
...WE CAN MAKE YOU A BUN CYBORG.
WE CANNOT LOSE SHIMA-RIN'S BUN OF JUSTICE.
NOT UNTIL ALL EVIL IS EX-PUNGED FROM THIS WORLD...
I HAVE NO IDEA WHAT'S GOING ON ANY-MORE.
MY SENPAI ARE SO WEIRD...

PHEW...
THAT FEELS SO NICE.
SHORT HAIR IS SO MUCH EASIER TO WASH.
I'M OUT.
OH, RIN.
YOUR CELL PHONE RANG EARLI-ER.
OH, IT DID?

OH, IT WAS TAKEDA-SAN.
HELLO?
IT'S SHIMA. SORRY FOR MISSING YOUR CALL.
Ohh, Rin-chan, I'm sorry for calling so late.
I'M CALLING ABOUT YOUR WORK SCHEDULE FOR GOLDEN WEEK.
THIS YEAR, FROM THE 2ND TO THE 6TH...
...I AM PLANNING TO CLOSE THE SHOP.
Close the shop?
SORRY! THERE'S A REASON, THOUGH. IN FEBRUARY, MY GRANDCHILD WAS BORN.
BUT THEY LIVE FAR AWAY, SO I HAVEN'T GOTTEN TO SEE THEM.
I'M THINKING OF GOING TO SEE THEM WITH MY WIFE OVER GOLDEN WEEK...
...WHICH WILL LEAVE NO ONE TO MANAGE THE SHOP.
I see.

I DO PLAN TO OPEN UP ON THE 30TH AND THE 1ST.
COULD YOU WORK THOSE TWO DAYS?
Yes, I can.
HMNN.
I WAS PLANNING ON WORKING ALL THROUGH GOLDEN WEEK...
WHY ARE YOU WEARING MY BUNS?

PEKON
ペコン
PEKON (BEEDOOP)
ペコン
道の駅
伊良湖
PEKON
ペコン
21:35
Last week, I went camping on the Atsumi Peninsula.

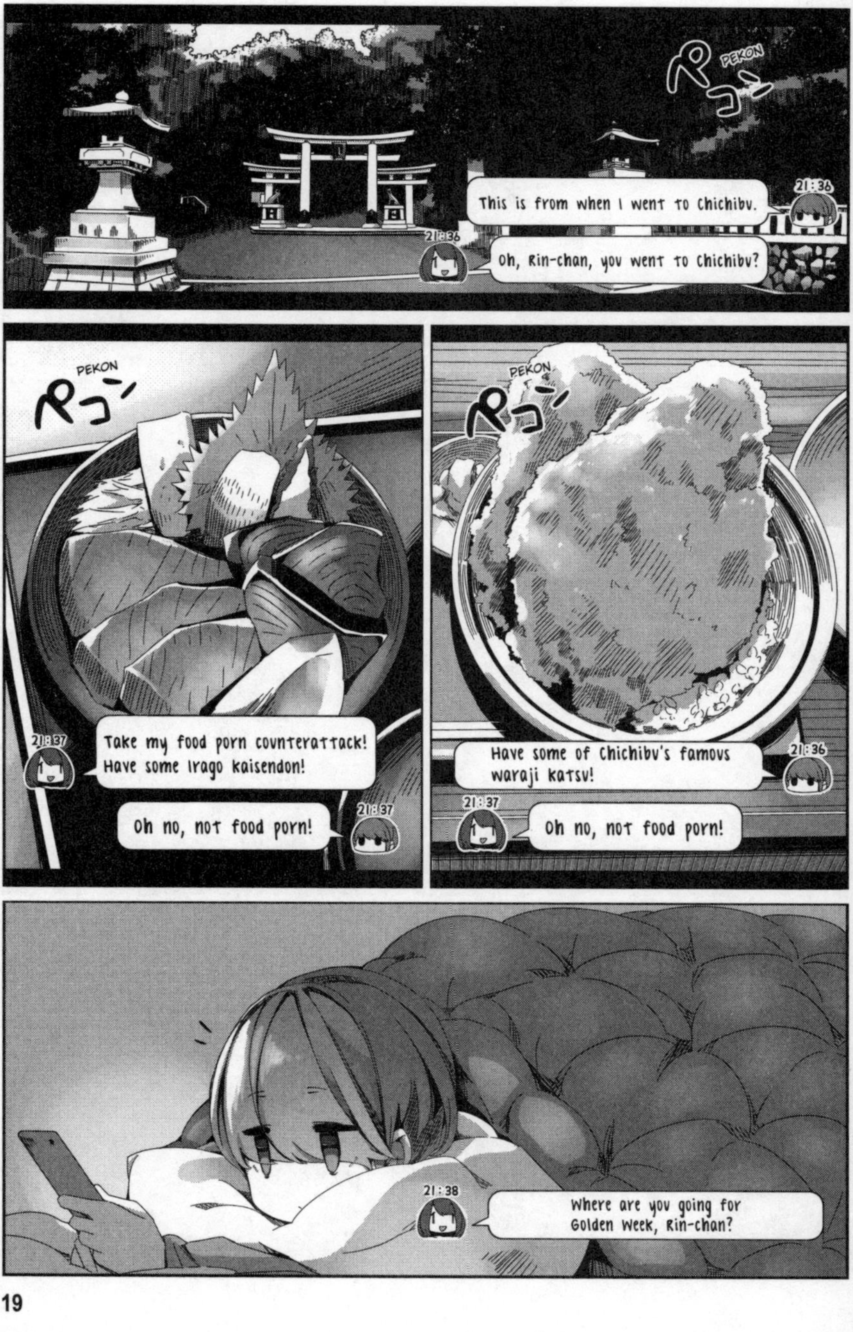
ペコン
PEKON
21:36
This is from when I went to Chichibu.
21:36
Oh, Rin-chan, you went to Chichibu?
ペコン
PEKON
Have some of Chichibu's famous waraji katsu!
21:36
21:37
Oh no, not food porn!
ペコン
PEKON
21:37
Take my food porn counterattack! Have some Irago kaisendon!
Oh no, not food porn!
21:37
21:38
Where are you going for Golden Week, Rin-chan?

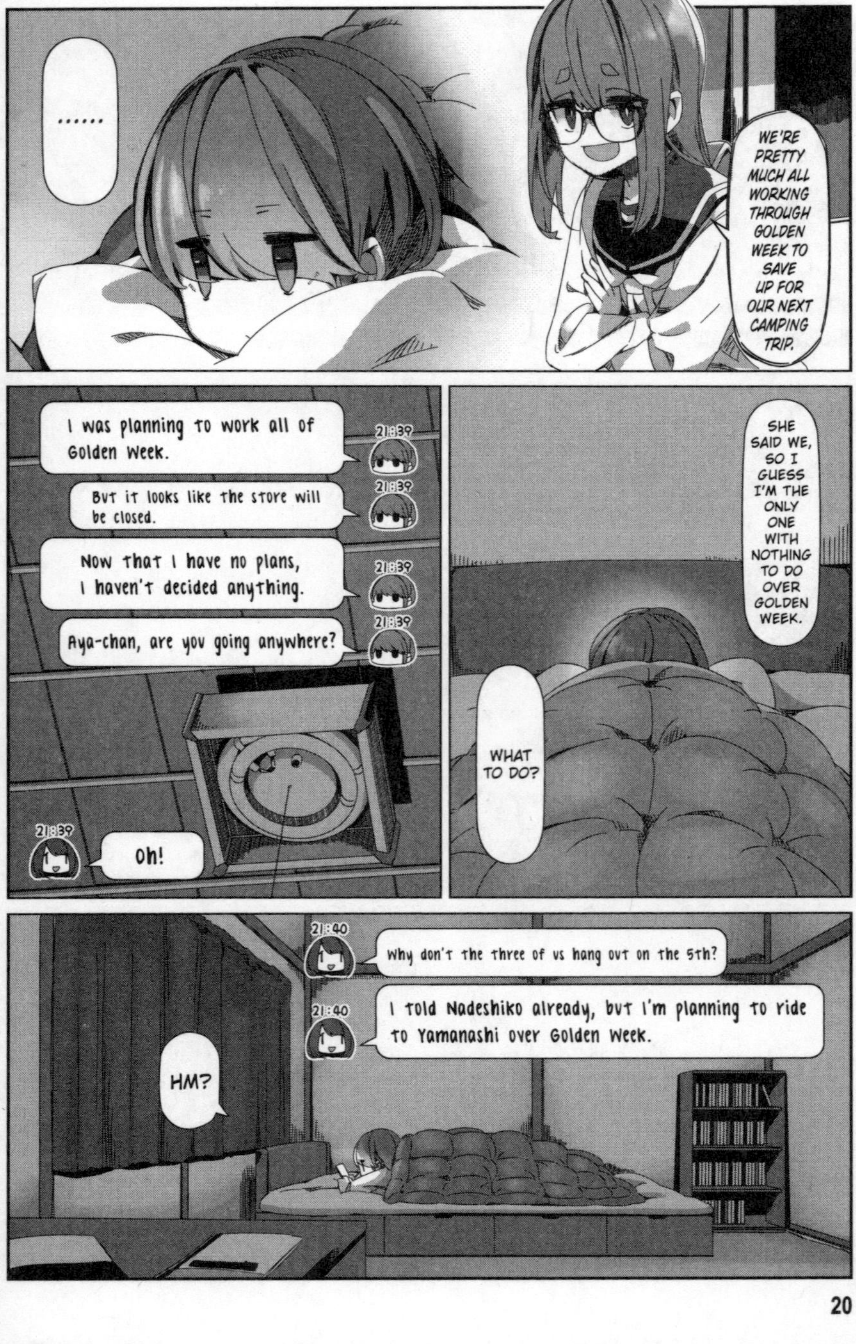
WE'RE PRETTY MUCH ALL WORKING THROUGH GOLDEN WEEK TO SAVE UP FOR OUR NEXT CAMPING TRIP.
......
SHE SAID WE, SO I GUESS I'M THE ONLY ONE WITH NOTHING TO DO OVER GOLDEN WEEK.
WHAT TO DO?
21:39
I was planning to work all of Golden Week.
21:39
But it looks like the store will be closed.
21:39
Now that I have no plans, I haven't decided anything.
21:39
Aya-chan, are you going anywhere?
21:39
Oh!
21:40
Why don't the three of us hang out on the 5th?
21:40
I told Nadeshiko already, but I'm planning to ride to Yamanashi over Golden Week.
HM?

AYA-CHAN'S COMING TO YAMAZAKI.
FINALLY.
DOES THAT MEAN NADE-SHIKO IS TAKING OFF ON THE FIFTH?
4G 75%
21:41
I see. The 5th, eh.
21:41
National Route 1 will probably be a rough ride still, so be careful.
21:42
Hm?
21:42
Oh, no.
21:42
I'm heading north via Hamamatsu and passing through Suwa to get to Yamanashi this time.
21:42
Oh, really?
LAKE SUWA
INA
KOMAGANE
152
20
52
YAMANASHI PREFECTURE
21:42
The route is National Route 152.
21:43
A friend from school told me about it.
21:43
Apparently it's a heck of a ride.

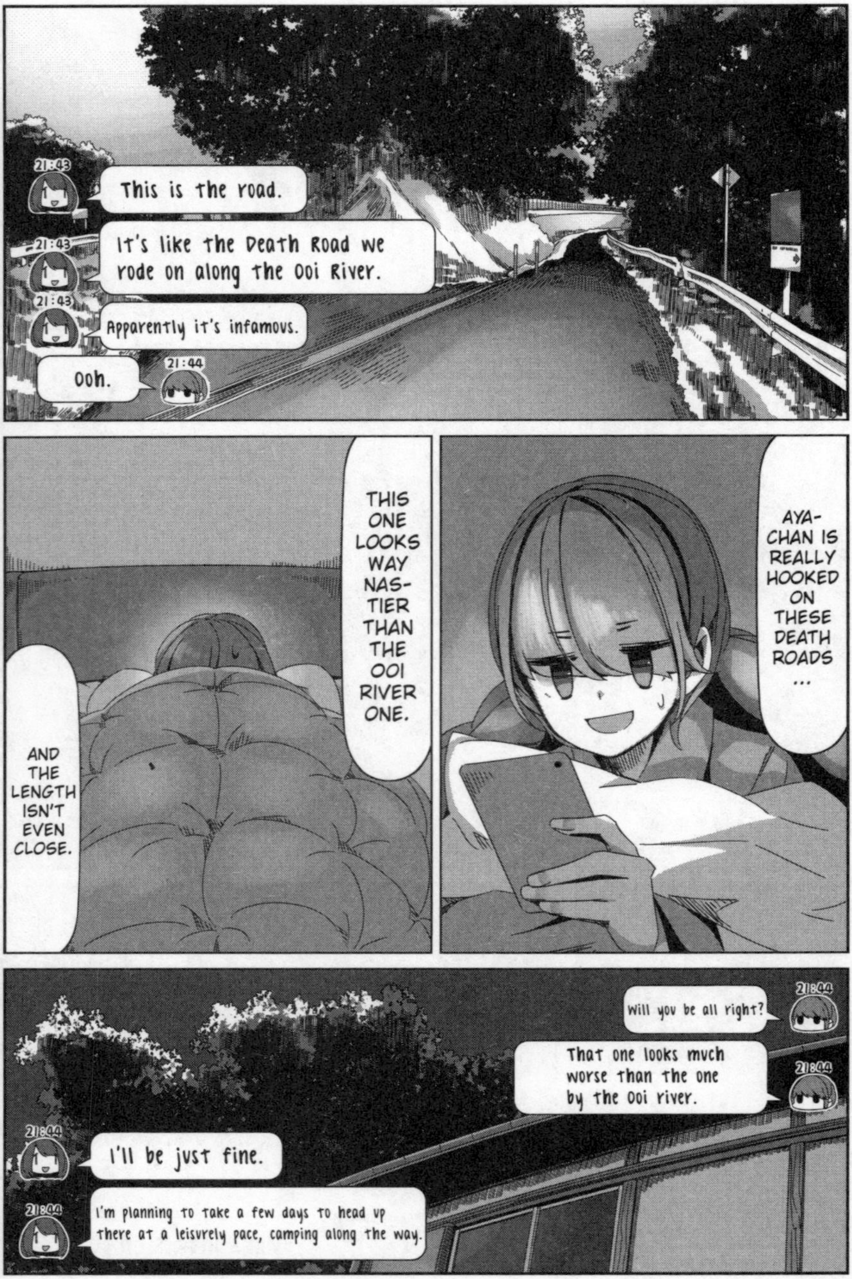

21:43
This is the road.
21:43
It's like the Death Road we rode on along the Ooi River.
21:43
Apparently it's infamous.
21:44
Ooh.
AYA-CHAN IS REALLY HOOKED ON THESE DEATH ROADS...
THIS ONE LOOKS WAY NASTIER THAN THE OOI RIVER ONE.
AND THE LENGTH ISN'T EVEN CLOSE.
21:44
Will you be all right?
21:44
That one looks much worse than the one by the Ooi river.
21:44
I'll be just fine.
21:44
I'm planning to take a few days to head up there at a leisurely pace, camping along the way.

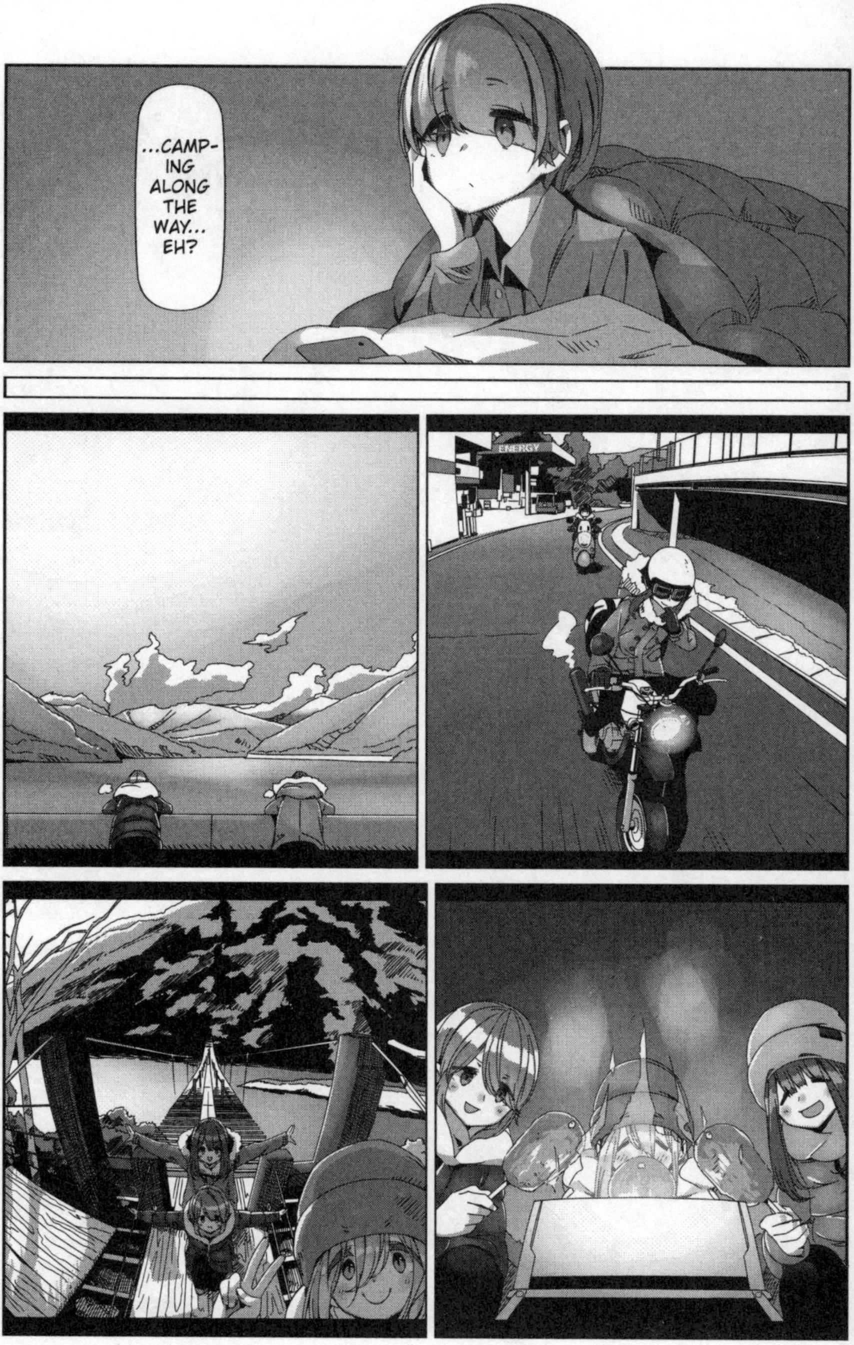
...CAMP-
ING
ALONG
THE
WAY...
EH?
ENERGY

21:46
I think I've changed my mind.
21:46
Can I ride with you?

SO SLEEPY ...

GIII
(CREEEAK)
BUMP
WHY'RE YOU SLEEPING OUT HERE?
ZZZZZZ...

SHIMA RIN
THAT IS DEFINITELY NOT ME!

YOU CAN HIDE THINGS INSIDE.
PERFECT FOR SHURIKEN OR CALTROPS.

KIINKOON (DIING-DOONG)
キーンコーン
カーンコーン
KAANKOON (DAANG-DOONG)
IT TOOK A LOT OF TIME TO DO ALL THIS RE-SEARCH ...
...BUT THE PLANS FOR DAY ONE ARE DONE.
Sketch Note
NOW, WHAT TO DO ABOUT DAY TWO ...?
HMMM...
SINCE WE'RE GOING TO GUNMA, I'D LIKE TO CAMP SOME-WHERE AT LEAST ONE NIGHT.
I SHOULD GO ASK RIN-CHAN.
たっ TA (TMP)
たっ TA

CHAPTER 89 NADESHIKO'S GUNMA SOLO-CAMP PLAN

IT SOUNDS LIKE SHIMA-SAN HAS WORK TODAY.
OH, I SEE.
I DID WANT RIN-CHAN'S OPINION.
OH WELL.
NADE-SHIKO-CHAN, NADE-SHIKO-CHAN!
Sketch Note
HEEEY!
HELLO, ENA-CHAN.
IS SOMETHING THE MATTER?
OH, YEAH. I WAS COMING TO SEE RIN-CHAN.
HELLO.
HELLO.
OH, HELLO, EMA-CHAN.

I WAS PUTTING TO-GETHER A PLAN TO GO SOLO CAMPING IN GUNMA FOR GOLDEN WEEK.
Sketch Note
I WANTED TO GET HER ADVICE.
WOW, GUNMA.
CAN I SEE?
TOTALLY.
OOH, LOOKS LIKE FUN.
THIS MUST HAVE TAKEN A LOT OF WORK.
IT DID. I WAS UP LAST NIGHT THINKING ABOUT HOW I WOULD GET THERE.
NAGANO PREFECTURE
CHANGE TRAINS HERE
TAKE THE BUS FROM HERE
KYAA!
ABT ROAD
KARUIZAWA
TWISTY, TURNY ROAD
GET OFF HERE.
GASHUNK GASHUNK
GOLDEN WEEK
GUNMA SOLO CAMP DAY 1
DAY 1 CAMP SITE
GOAL
FOREST CAFE
HOT SPRING
LAKE USUI
YOKOKAWA RAIL MUSEUM
KOUFU
HOME
GET ON HERE
MT. FUJI
GUNMA PREFECTURE
TAKE THE TRAIN AGAIN HERE
CHANGE TRAINS HERE
VROOM

TSUGATAKE
GASHUNK GASHUNK
KOUMI LINE
GREAT VIEW OF YATSUGATAKE FROM THE EAST-FACING WINDOWS!!
I'LL START OUT HEADING THROUGH NAGANO BY TRAIN TO KARUIZAWA.
CHANGE TRAINS HERE.
THE SIGHT FROM THE TRAIN AS IT PASSES IN FRONT OF YATSUGATAKE...
...IS SUPPOSED TO BE BEAUTIFUL.
OOOH.
WHEN I REACH KARUIZAWA, I'LL TAKE A BUS...
MEGANE BRIDGE
YEEK!
TAKE THE BUS FROM HERE.
KARUIZAWA
KUMANOTAIRA
GET OFF HERE.
TWISTY, TURNY ROAD
THE BUS WILL TAKE ME TO THE PARKING LOT IN KUMANOTAIRA.
FROM THERE, I CAN TAKE A LEISURELY STROLL ON THE ABANDONED TRACKS TURNED INTO A FOOTPATH.
STOP AND SHOP AT THIS GROCERY STORE
TO TOWN HALL
CHECK-IN
FOREST CAFÉ
LAKE USUI
MOUNTAIN HOT SPRING
ABT ROAD
HERE YOU CAN WALK ALONG THE ABANDONED REMAINS OF ABT RAILROAD TRACKS. 6KM LONG FOOTPATH.
YOU CAN HIKE HERE.
MEGANE BRIDGE
KYAA!
KUMANOTAIRA GET OFF HERE.
I NEVER KNEW THIS ROUTE EXISTED.

I PLAN TO TAKE MY TIME MAKING MY WAY TO YOKO-KAWA...
...WHILE STOPPING OFF AT PLACES LIKE MEGANE BRIDGE, THE FOREST CAFÉ, AND THE MOUNTAIN HOT SPRINGS.
ONCE I GET TO YOKO-KAWA, I'LL EAT THEIR FAMOUS KAMA-MESHI.
AND WITH MY TUMMY FULL, WALK AROUND AND SEE THE EX-HIBITS.
CAN'T-MISS LOCAL CUISINE
OH, I'VE HEARD OF THEIR KAMA-MESHI.
THE TRUTH IS, MY WHOLE REASON FOR PLANNING THIS TRIP IS FOR THE YOKO-KAWA RAIL MUSEUM.
I SEE.
THEN, AFTER I GET MY FILL OF THE MUSEUM, I'LL HEAD TOWARD TAKA-SAKI BY TRAIN.
VROOM
GUNMA-SOJA
TAKE THE BUS FROM HERE.
GASHUNK GASHUNK
TAKASAKI
THEN I'LL CATCH AN-OTHER BUS.
CHANGE TRAINS HERE.

I'LL GO SHOPPING ALONG THE WAY, THEN HEAD FOR THE CAMP-SITE...
DAY 1
CAMP SITE
GOAL
FINAL SPURT!
THE HILL CLIMB TO THE CAMPSITE
FINAL BUS STOP
CAFÉ
...NEAR IKAHO HOT SPRINGS, AND THAT'S DAY ONE.
THIS CAMPSITE REQUIRES RESER-VATION BY SNAIL MAIL AND THAT YOU ARRIVE THE DAY OF TO APPLY IN PERSON AT TOWN HALL.
IT SEEM TO BE A REAL HIDDEN GEM, BUT THAT'S PROBABLY 'COS THE RESERVATION PROCESS IS SO HARD.
EVEN FINDING IT WAS TOUGH.
Sketch Note
NADE-SHIKO-CHAN, THIS HAS ME WON-DERING ...
WILL YOU MAKE IT IN TIME FOR CHECK-IN?
EH?

C-COME TO THINK OF IT, LAST NIGHT...
THIS IS PERFECT.
I THINK I MIGHT HAVE ONLY DECIDED UPON THE ROUTE ITSELF BEFORE DOZING OFF...
07:52 DEPARTS — 13:17 ARRIVES
TRAVEL TIME: 3H25M
TRANSFERS: 3
DEPARTURE
DEPARTS 07:52 UTSUBUNA
MINOBU LINE KOUFU LIN
ARRIVES 09:21 DEPARTS 09:29 KOUFU
CHUO MAIN LINE MINAM
ARRIVES 09:53 DEPARTS 10:07 KOBUCHIZAWA
KOUMI LINE KOMOR
:19 :52 KOMORO
HOKUSHIN RAILWAY KARU
INATION
KARUIZAWA
LOOK.
EVEN IF YOU CATCH THE EARLIEST BUS FROM UTSUBUNA, IT'LL BE AFTER ONE P.M. WHEN YOU GET THERE.
WHOA! IT TAKES THAT LONG!?
B-BUT CHECK-IN'S IN THE EVENING, SO IF I WALK THE ABT ROAD QUICKLY, I SHOULD MAKE IT...
IF I PSYCH MYSELF UP...
KAGAMIHARA-SENPAI.
THE BUS TO THE ABT ROAD ONLY COMES ONCE A DAY, AND IT LEAVES AT 12:55.
BUROROROROR (VRRRROOOOM)
SO THAT'S COMPLETELY OUT...
PACKED ITINERARY

WHICH MEANS SHE HAS TO CHANGE HER PLANS.
HOW ABOUT THIS?
HMM.
SIGN: KARUIZAWA STATION
SIGN: KOUFU STATION
FIRST, HEAD TO KOUFU STATION BY CAR.
CIERO
甲府駅
FROM THERE, TAKE THE FIRST TRAIN TO KARUIZAWA.
YOU'LL LOSE TIME WAITING FOR A BUS.
BURORORORO (VRRRROOOOM)
ブロロロロ
SO TAKE A TAXI TO KUMANOTAIRA FROM KARUIZAWA STATION.

SAKA (HIKE) せか
SAKA せか
ONCE YOU REACH THE ABT ROAD...
...WALK IT QUICKLY WITHOUT ANY STOPS UNTIL THE END...
...SEE EVERY-THING AT THE MUSEUM IN 30 MINUTES...
SEKA せか
SEKA せか
SEKA せか
FAAAAAN (HOOOOONK) ファーーン
...CATCH THE 1:10 P.M. TRAIN BOUND FOR TAKA-SAKI...
...AND THEN YOU SHOULD MAKE IT IN TIME FOR CHECK-IN, I THINK.
SEEMS LIKE YOUR FUN HIKING TRIP HAS BECOME ENDURANCE TRAINING.
WELL, YOU COULD TAKE A TAXI AND SKIP THE ABT ROAD...
...AND JUST GO STRAIGHT TO THE EXHIBIT. WOULD THAT BE BETTER?
I THINK THAT WAY, YOU'LL HAVE MORE TIME.
FOREST CAFÉ
MEGANE BRIDGE
BUUUU (BEEEEEP)
LAKE USUI
MOUNTAIN HOT SPRING
UMANO TAIRA
GET OFF HERE.
SKIPPING ALL OF THIS

THEN YOU COULD TAKE YOUR TIME TOURING THE EXHIBIT.
SO I WOULD HAVE TO SKIP THE ENTIRE ABT ROAD?
HRRNH.
SINCE I'LL BE THERE ALREADY, I WANNA TRY WALKING THE WHOLE ROAD...
...BUT I ALSO WANNA TAKE MY TIME AND SEE THE EXHIBIT ...
I'LL HAVE TO MULL THIS PART OVER SOME MORE ...
THAT SEEMS BEST.
HOW ABOUT DAY TWO?
WELL.
I THOUGHT I'D GO TO THE IKAHO HOT SPRINGS.
IT IS NEAR THE CAMP-SITE.

I'M STILL THINKING OVER THE REST.
I'M HAVING A HARD TIME FINDING CAMPSITES THAT WOULD LIKELY HAVE OPENINGS.
WELL, IT *IS* GOLDEN WEEK.
NADESHIKO-CHAN, WHEN ARE YOU GOING CAMPING IN GUNMA?
I'M THINKING MAY 2ND THROUGH THE 4TH.
FROM THE 2ND TO THE 4TH, EH?
CAN I COME TOO?
OH, YOU WANNA JOIN ME, ENA-CHAN?

HEARING YOU TALK ABOUT IT MAKES ME WANNA GO.
AND I'M FREE THE BACK HALF OF GOLDEN WEEK.
YES, COME WITH ME!
OH.
SENPAI.
I KNOW OF ONE CAMPSITE IN GUNMA...
...THAT WILL LIKELY HAVE OPENINGS DURING GOLDEN WEEK.
WHOA!! IT'S SO PRETTY!
THERE'S A CAMPSITE THERE?
YES.

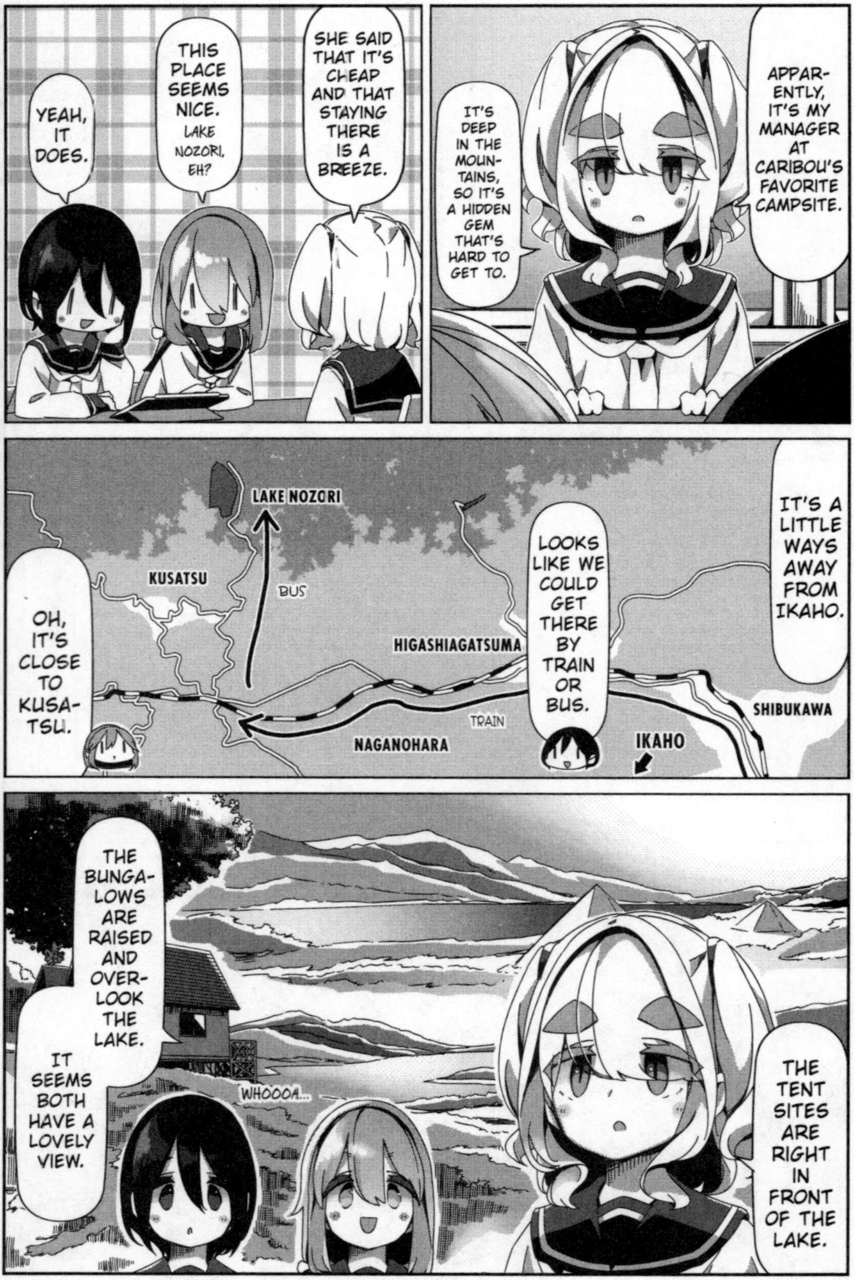
APPARENTLY, IT'S MY MANAGER AT CARIBOU'S FAVORITE CAMPSITE.
IT'S DEEP IN THE MOUNTAINS, SO IT'S A HIDDEN GEM THAT'S HARD TO GET TO.
SHE SAID THAT IT'S CHEAP AND THAT STAYING THERE IS A BREEZE.
THIS PLACE SEEMS NICE.
LAKE NOZORI, EH?
YEAH, IT DOES.
IT'S A LITTLE WAYS AWAY FROM IKAHO.
LOOKS LIKE WE COULD GET THERE BY TRAIN OR BUS.
OH, IT'S CLOSE TO KUSATSU.
LAKE NOZORI
KUSATSU
BUS
HIGASHIAGATSUMA
SHIBUKAWA
TRAIN
NAGANOHARA
IKAHO
THE TENT SITES ARE RIGHT IN FRONT OF THE LAKE.
THE BUNGALOWS ARE RAISED AND OVERLOOK THE LAKE.
IT SEEMS BOTH HAVE A LOVELY VIEW.
WHOOOA...

ALSO, I HEARD THERE'S SOME-THING REAL SPECIAL TO EAT AT THE AREA ACROSS THE LAKE...
FRESH, HANDMADE PIZZA WITH WILD PLANTS ...
OOH...
EMA-CHAN.
HUH!?
NIKO
NIKO (BEAM)
DO YOU... WANNA CAMP WITH US?
NIKO
NIKO

WOW, EMA-CHAN.
YOU'RE GOING TO LAKE NOZORI FOR YOUR FIRST CAMPING TRIP.
YES.
AN UPPER-CLASSMAN AT MY HIGH SCHOOL MADE PLANS TO GO CAMPING N GUNMA OVER GOLDEN WEEK.
WHILE WE WERE TALKING IT OVER, SHE INVITED ME.
SO I WANTED TO BORROW SOME CAMPING GEAR... MAY I?
Yes, of course!
HOW ARE YOU GETTING TO GUNMA? BY CAR?
By train and bus.
WHICH MEANS YOU'LL BE DOING SOME WALKING.

So lighter gear meant for mountain climbing would probably be best.
You'll need a tent, sleeping bag...
Oh yeah! It's the beginning of May, so nights at Lake Nozori get pretty cold. Will you be okay?
Oh! Do they?
Yes. The road closure for winter has only just ended, after all.
There may even still be snow on the ground.
Ohh...
Naturally I'll lend you my cold weather sleeping bag I use in winter...
...but I also think you all should stay in a bungalow.

YOU COULD BE IN TROUBLE IF YOU ALL DON'T HAVE WINTER GEAR.
CHECK WITH THE OTHERS YOU'RE GOING WITH.
I-I will.
20:15 Looks like Lake Nozori is really cold at night during Golden Week.
20:15 Do you two have winter sleeping bags and stuff?
20:18 I checked the weather for Lake Nozori.
20:18 Locks like it's still wintry there.
PEKON (BEEDOOP)
ペコン
20:18 But we should be all right. We started camping in winter after all.
OH GOOD, I'M GLAD.
20:18 I have a winter sleeping bag.
20:18 I have one too.
PEKON
ペコン
20:18 But we camped at Lake Yamanaka in January, the dead of winter.
WHAT!?
20:18 I thought I was gonna die.
PEKON
ペコン

20:19
We were in a rough spot. Shimarin-sama came to our rescue.
20:19
Yes, we must thank that Shimarin-sama.
20:19
We were also saved by Sensei and the great canine and the liquor store people.
20:19
The great canine was so cute.
20:20
I'm sorry, I don't really get what you're talking about, but let's get a bungalow so we don't freeze.
20:20
All right.
IBIKAWA-SAN IS LENDING ME CAMPING GEAR.
I BETTER PACK SOME WARM CLOTHES ...

OUTSIDE OF LAKE NOZORI, EVERY-WHERE ELSE WILL HAVE EARLY SUMMER TEMPS ...
I GUESS I COULD BRING DOWN OR FLEECE THAT I CAN FOLD UP EASILY.
OH, AND MONEY FOR TRAVEL FARE.
MAYBE I SHOULD BORROW SOME FROM MOM.
WHAT !?
RIN-CHAN!
NADE-SHIKO!
YOU'RE OFF WORK FOR GOLDEN WEEK!?

AWW!
If I had known you were off, I would have invited you to camp with us.
IT SEEMS THE MANAGER HAS SOME-THING, AND IS CLOSING THE SHOP.
You're going to Gunma, right?
YEAH.
MY ORIGINAL PLAN WAS SOLO CAMP-ING.
BUT NOW ENA-CHAN AND EMA-CHAN ARE COMING TOO.
Oh, Mizu-nami-san is going too?
RIN-CHAN, YOU'RE GOING TOURING WITH AYA-CHAN, RIGHT?
We're gonna ride on another Death Road.
YOU REALLY LIKE THOSE, HUH?
You two'll be here on the night of the 4th, right?
WE'LL DO OUR BEST TO MAKE THAT DATE.
WHAT ABOUT YOU?
I plan to be back that night.

THEN WE CAN SWAP STORIES ABOUT OUR TRIPS.
YEAH.
MAY 2 6:20 AM

GOOD MORNING.
G-GOOD MORNING.
SUKAAAA (ZZZZZZZ)
すや
NADESHIKO, WE'RE AT KOUFU STATION.
SO EXCITED, SHE DIDN'T SLEEP MUCH
BWEEEEEH.
NOT A MORNING PERSON

GOOD MORNING.
MIZU-NAMI-SAN... RIGHT?
UH, YES.
WIDE AWAKE
GOOD LUCK WITH THOSE TWO.
ず
い
ZU I (ZOOM)
WHA ...?

NOZORI
PIZZA...

I MAY BE A CUTE DRAWING ON THE SKETCH-BOOK MAP...
...BUT IF YOU MEET ME ON THE ABT ROAD, I'LL BE A PICTURE OF PAIN.

SIGN: KARUIZAWA STATION

CHAPTER 90
KARUIZAWA FOR ONE MOMENT—THE NEXT, GUNMA

H-HOW!?
BUT WE JUST GOT ON THE TRAIN AT KOUFU STATION BOUND FOR MATSU-MOTO...
DID WE WARP??
YOU REALLY ARE STILL HALF-ASLEEP...
KATATAN (GASHUNSHUNG)
ガタタン
ガタタン
KATATAN
KATATAN
ガタタン
KAGAMI-HARA-SENPAI, THERE'S YATSU-GATAKE.
NMHM, REALLY?
KATATAN
ガタタン
KATATAN
ガタタン
LOOK HOW PRETTY, ENA-CHAN.
SUPIII (ZZZZZ)
スピー
OH YEAHHH. SO YUMMY.
KATATAN
ガタタン

●REC
WOW, THERE WE ARE, RIDING THE KOUMI LINE.
I TOOK PLENTY OF VIDEOS AND PHOTOS OF THE VIEW FROM THE KOUMI LINE.
TH-THANK YOU...
ALSO, I ALREADY CALLED FOR A TAXI, SO THEY SHOULD BE WAITING DOWN BELOW.
O-OH, OKAY.
SAITOU-SENPAI, LET'S HEAD TO THE TAXI STAND.
UH-HUH...
SHE'S SUCH A CAPABLE UNDERCLASSMAN...

TAXI CALLED FOR...
...BY MY CAPABLE JUNIOR.
YAY!
SIGN: NO ENTRY
UMM, PLEASE TAKE US TO THE CAFÉ IN FRONT OF LAKE USUI.
進入禁止
OHH, CLUBMAN, RIGHT?
THAT'S RIGHT.
OH!
ARE YOU ALL GOING CAMPING?
OH, YES.

WOW, SO YOU'RE GOING TO WALK THE ABT ROAD FROM LAKE USUI TO YOKO-KAWA?
ブロロロロ
BURORORORO (VRRRRROOOOM)
I REALLY WANTED TO WALK FROM KUMA-NOTAIRA TO YOKO-KAWA...
...BUT I'D NEVER MAKE THE TRAIN IN TIME.
I SEE. SO YOU CHOSE TO START FROM LAKE USUI INSTEAD.
群馬県
Gunma Pref.
安中市
Annaka City
AH.
SENPAI, LOOKS LIKE WE'RE EN-TERING GUNMA.
OH!

群馬県
Gunma Pref.
安中市
Annaka City
OOH, WE'RE IN GUNMA!
WE ARE.
A NAME LIKE THAT MAKES ME WANNA EAT ANKO MONAKA WAFERS ...
I REALLY DON'T FOLLOW ...
群馬県
Gunma Pref.
安中市
Annaka City
WOW.
ANNAKA CITY, EH?
WHOA!
BURORORO

WHOA...
WHOOOA!
BUROROROROM (VRRRRROOOOM)
ブロロロロー
THIS ROAD SURE HAS LOTS OF TWISTS AND TURNS.
I NOTICED WHEN LOOKING AT THE MAP, BUT THIS ROAD REALLY IS SOMETHING.
↑ 熊ノ平駐車場
350m Kumanotaira Parking
GUNMA
WE'LL BE AT THE KUMANOTAIRA PARKING LOT SHORTLY.
BURORORORO
ブロロロロー
EMA-CHAN, ARE YOU ALL RIGHT WITH ALL THE TURNS?
I-I'M FINE.

LOTS OF FOLKS PARK HERE...
...AND HEAD FOR THE ABT ROAD.
I SEE.
WOULD YOU LIKE TO GO SEE THE OLD ABAN-DONED STATION, SINCE WE'RE HERE?
CAN WE?
IF THE CAB IS STOPPED TOO LONG, THE METER WILL RUN...
...BUT IF YOU TAKE A QUICK PEEK, YOU SHOULD BE FINE.
THANK YOU SO MUCH!
KUMANOTAIRA PARKING

I'M GONNA GO TAKE A LOOK AT THE OLD ABANDONED STATION.
ガチャ
GACHA (KACHAK)
WHAT ABOUT YOU, EMA-CHAN?
I'LL COME TOO...
ENA-CHAN...
ZZZZZ...
...IS STILL ASLEEP.
SNAP

WE BETTER HURRY AND GO LOOK.
RIGHT.

WHOA...
THIS IS THE ABT RACK SECTION OF THE OLD KUMANO-TAIRA STATION.
IT WAS AN USUI DISTRICT RAILWAY STATION THAT SERVED THE SHIN'ETSU MAIN LINE OF THE JAPAN NATIONAL RAILWAYS IN THE FORMER TOWN OF MATSUIDA.
THIS STATION WAS BUILT OVER A HUNDRED YEARS AGO.
KASHA (SNAP)
KASHA
KASHA
IT HAS SUCH PRESENCE.

KUMANOTAIRA
FOREST CAFE
MEGANE BRIDGE
LAKE USUI
ABANDONED POWER STATION
MOUNTAIN HOT SPRING
YOKOKAWA RAIL MUSEUM
THE ABT ROAD ACTUALLY STARTS IN YOKO-KAWA...
...WITH THIS BEING THE FINAL STOP...
BUT BECAUSE WE'RE STARTING HERE...
...IT'LL BE ALL DOWN-HILL. MUCH EASIER.
EASIER IS BETTER.
EMA-CHAN.
LET'S TAKE A PIC TO RE-MEMBER THIS MOMENT BY.
OH, OKAY.
SNAP
NOW, LET'S COMBINE THAT WITH THE ONE WE TOOK EARLIER OF ENA-CHAN...

THERE!!
IT'S LIKE SHE'S ABSENT FOR A GRAD-UATION PHOTO.
SORRY FOR MAKING YOU WAIT.
OH, NOT AT ALL.
SHALL WE STOP BY MEGANE BRIDGE AS WELL?
THERE'S A POP-ULAR TOURIST SPOT AROUND HERE.

BUROROROROROO (VRRRROOOOM)
ブロロロロー
← 熊ノ平駐車場
YES, PLEASE !!
I SEE— SO YOU'RE HEADED TO CAMP AT LAKE NOZORI TOMORROW. THAT FAR, EH?
YEP, YEP!
TRUTH IS, I QUITE LIKE CAMPING MYSELF.
WHEN MY KIDS WERE LITTLE, WE OFTEN WENT CAMPING ON MT. AKAGI AND MT. HARUNA.
BOTH ARE LAKESIDE CAMPSITES AND ARE REAL NICE.
WITH AKAGI IN PARTICULAR, SINCE IT'S FREE TO CAMP THERE...
...YOU CAN NEVER GET A RESERVATION.
WOW.

WE'RE PLAN-NING TO STOP AT MT. HARUNA TOMOR-ROW.
THAT SO?
THE VIEW FROM THE PEAK THERE IS GOR-GEOUS.
IF YOU HAVE TIME, PLEASE TRY GOING TO THE TOP VIA THE ROPEWAY.
AH.
YOU CAN SEE MEGANE BRIDGE THERE.
ブロロロロー
BUROROROROR
(VRRRROOOOM)
WOW, IT'S—
WAY BIGGER THAN I EX-PECTED.
RIGHT?

FWAAAAHHH!
SORRY, SORRY. I GUESS I NODDED OFF FOR A BIT.
ARE WE AT KOUFU STATION YET?
WE'RE IN GUNMA.
EH?
HANG ON.
WE JUST GOT TO YOUR HOUSE, EMA-CHAN.
OVER THERE IS USUI'S MEGANE BRIDGE.

MEGANE BRIDGE
IT'S MEGANE BRIDGE.
......
YAAAY! GUNMA ROCKS!!

ENJOY YOUR TRAVELS HERE IN GUNMA.
YES-SIR!
THANK YOU VERY MUCH.
BUROROROROO (VRRRROOOOM)
ブロロロロ
WHEW.
I'M SO GLAD WE SPLIT THAT CAB FARE.
SO THANKFUL.
TO THINK YOU WERE ORIGI-NALLY GONNA COME ALONE.
IT'S 10:43 NOW.
WE CAN RELAX A BIT AT THE CAFÉ UNTIL ELEVEN.
THEN WALK THE ABT ROAD UNTIL THE FAR-THEST POINT, WHICH SHOULD TAKE US UNTIL NOON.
OOH, DOGGY!
OPEN
CAFE

SIGN: YOKOKAWA RAIL MUSEUM
横川鉄道博物館
THE TRAIN BOUND FOR TAKA-SAKI LEAVES AT 1:10 P.M.
SO THAT SHOULD GIVE US AN HOUR TO LOOK AROUND THE MUSEUM!
IS AN HOUR GOING TO BE ENOUGH?
I'M NOT REALLY THAT MUCH OF A TRAIN NERD.
HEH...
SO AN HOUR SHOULD BE JUST ENOUGH FOR A LOOK AROUND!!
SHE REALLY IS SLAP-DASH ABOUT EVERY-THING.
COFFEE·HOUSE CLUBMAN
HELLO...
KARAN (JANGLE) カラン カラン KARAN

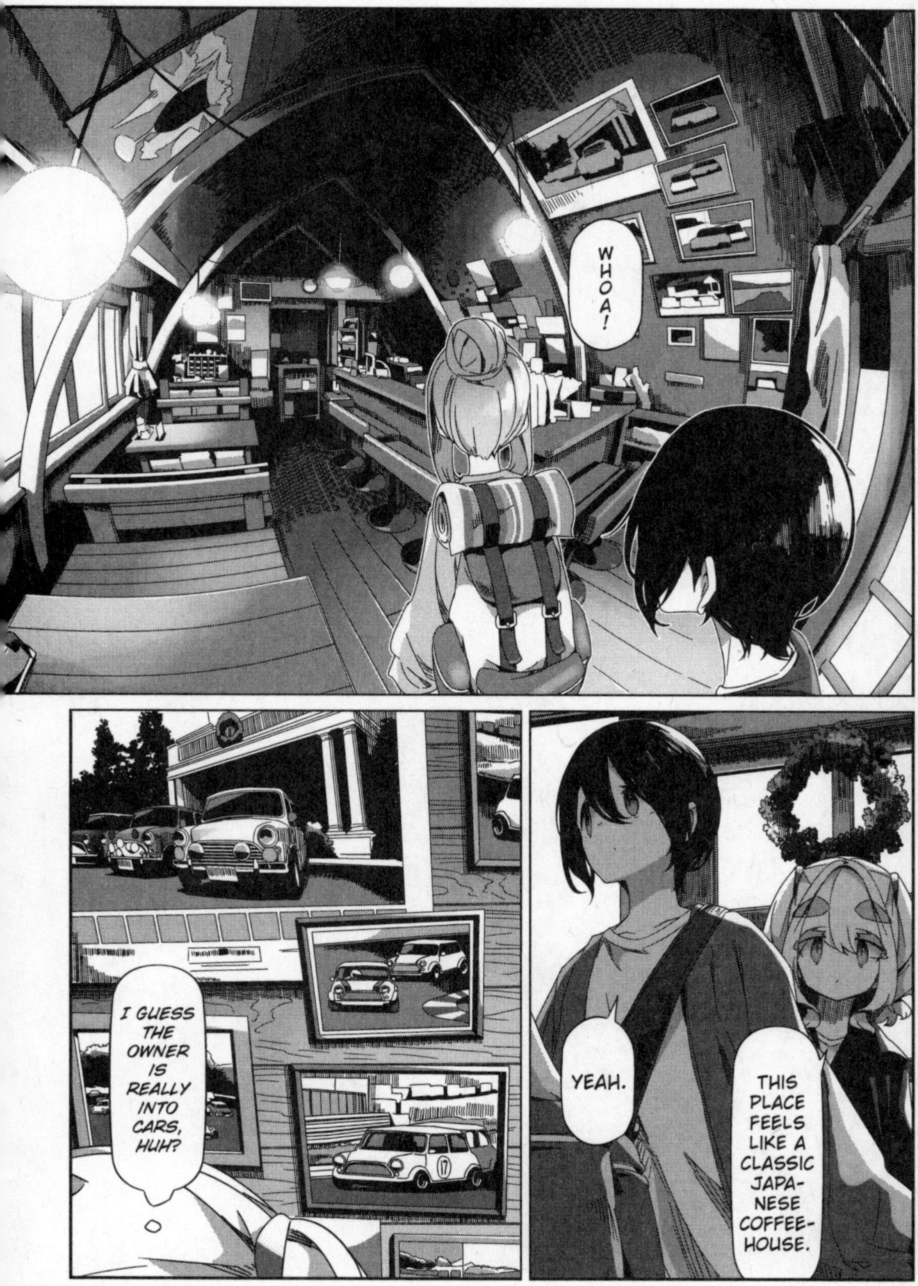
WHOA!
THIS PLACE FEELS LIKE A CLASSIC JAPANESE COFFEEHOUSE.
YEAH.
I GUESS THE OWNER IS REALLY INTO CARS, HUH?

OH, WELCOME.
PLEASE SIT WHEREVER YOU LIKE.
THANKS!
LET'S SEE. I'LL HAVE ...
...AN ICED COCOA, PLEASE.
I'LL HAVE AN ICED CAFÉ AU LAIT, PLEASE.
I'LL HAVE GINGER ALE.
ALL RIGHT, I'LL HAVE IT ALL OUT IN A JIFF.
WHEW.
IT WAS EXHAUSTING COMING ALL THIS WAY.
HOLD ON.
ENA-CHAN, YOU SLEPT ALMOST THE ENTIRE TRIP.

I'M SO GLAD WE CHANGED TRAINS AND CAUGHT THE SHINKANSEN AT SAKUDAIRA STATION.
OTHERWISE, THERE'S NO WAY WE'D BE TAKING A BREAK HERE.
ARRIVES AT 10:37
KARUIZAWA
KOMORO
ARRIVES AT 9:59
SAKUDAIRA
WE GOT HERE ALMOST FORTY MINUTES SOONER THAN...
...MY ORIGINAL PLAN TO TAKE THE KOUMI LINE ALL THE WAY TO KOMORO.
THOUGH IT WAS A LITTLE MORE EXPENSIVE.
BUT I DON'T REMEMBER THE SHINKANSEN OR THE KOUMI LINE, DO YOU?
I DON'T REMEMBER ANYTHING AFTER BEING IN MY DAD'S CAR!
EMA-CHAN, THANK YOU FOR LEADING US...
...ALL THE WAY HERE IN ONE PIECE!
I-IT'S FINE.

FAAAAN (HOOOONK)
WITHOUT YOU, WE MIGHT HAVE MISSED OUR STOP AND ENDED UP IN MATSUMOTO RIGHT ABOUT NOW.
OR WE MIGHT HAVE GOTTEN IT BACKWARD AND ENDED UP IN TOKYO.
I COULD SEE THAT.
BUT KAGAMIHARA-SENPAI, YOU SLEPT THROUGH THE RIDE ON THE KOUMI LINE.
EVEN THOUGH YOU SAID YOU WERE LOOKING FORWARD TO THE VIEW.
WE'LL BE TAKING THE KOUMI LINE ON THE WAY BACK, SO I CAN ENJOY THE VIEW PLENTY THEN.
I-IT'S FINE.
I SEE.
WHICH MEANS SHE'LL BE SO TIRED FROM OUR TRIP, SHE'LL FALL ASLEEP AGAIN.
N-NO I WON'T.
HA HA HA HA.

KANJI ON BOX: AN

SPEAKING OF YAMA-NASHI, I USED TO RIDE THE OYAMACHO CIRCUIT.
THERE WAS A BYPASS THAT WENT UP TO LAKE KAWA-GUCHI FROM KOUFU.
I WOULD OFTEN RIDE IT AT DAWN.
THAT ROAD IS NICE AND TWISTY...
... MAKING IT A BLAST TO DRIVE ON.
WOW
BEE BEE BEE BEE BEE BEEP
BEE BEE BEE BEE BEE BEEP
ALARM 11:00

I'M SORRY, BUT WE'RE WALKING THE ABT ROAD ...
...ALL THE WAY TO YOKO-KAWA, SO WE SHOULD BE GOING.
ずずずず
ZUZUZUZU
ずずずず
ZUZUZUZU (SSSSLURP)
OH! ARE YOU NOW?
THE DRINKS WERE GREAT!
OPEN
CAFE
BE SAFE ON YOUR WAY TO YOKO-KAWA.
THE OWNER OF THAT SHOP SURE LIKES CARS.
YEAH.
THAT CAR WITH THE ROUND LIGHTS WAS CUTE.
IF I GET A CAR DOWN THE LINE, I WANT ONE WITH ROUND LIGHTS.
ME TOO.

CHAPTER 91 THE ABANDONED ABT RAIL WALKING TRAIL

THE TRACKS ARE STILL THERE AROUND THE OLD KUMANO-TAIRA STATION.
IT LOOKED KIND OF LIKE THE RAIL LINE WAS ABANDONED, THOUGH...
BUT THIS AREA FEELS NO DIFFERENT THAN A NORMAL FOREST FOOTPATH.
YEAH.
REALLY?
BUT THESE TUNNELS SURE MAKE YOU FEEL THAT TRAINS USED TO RUN THROUGH THEM.
MAYBE THEY TOOK UP THE TRACKS THAT USED TO BE HERE?
HMMM.
I THINK IT'S MORE LIKELY THEY BURIED THEM.
IT SEEMS LIKE TOO MUCH WORK TO PULL UP ALL THOSE TRACKS.

SENPAI WAS RIGHT. IT'S DOWNHILL, SO IT'S AN EASY WALK.
ざっ ZA
ざっ ZA
ざっ ZA
ざっ ZA (SHF)
ガラ GARA (RATTLE)
ガラ GARA
UL AIR MATT
UL SLEEPING BAG
UL RUCKSACK
UL TENT
UL SMALLER ITEMS
MEAN-WHILE, WHAT I BORROWED FITS IN MY BACK-PACK.
BUT THEIR SLEEP-ING BAGS ARE SO BIG.
THE GEAR THAT IBIKAWA-SAN LOANED ME...
...IS SUPER-LIGHT, SO THAT MIGHT ALSO BE WHY.
IT'S ALMOST ALL ULTRA-LIGHT.

I DIDN'T REALLY LOOK, BUT MAYBE WHAT SHE LOANED ME WAS HIGH QUALITY.
ZA (SKFF) ざっ
I BETTER BE CAREFUL NOT TO BREAK ANY OF IT.
ざっ ZA
HELLO.
HELLO.
IT'S SO SE-RENE.
ISN'T IT?
I'M SO GLAD WE OPTED FOR A LEI-SURELY WALK. IT'S NICE AND COOL.
NADE-SHIKO-CHAN, AREN'T THOSE LEFT-OVER TRACKS?
HM!
WOW, YEAH! THIS METAL STICKING OUT SURE LOOKS LIKE IT'S FOR A RAILWAY.

SO YOUR HUNCH WAS RIGHT, EMA-CHAN.
THEY COVERED UP THE TRACKS AND CON-VERTED IT TO A WALKING PATH.
LOOKS THAT WAY.
WHEW.
WE'RE LEAVING, SAITOU-SENPAI.
AH, HOLD ON, WAIT!

中山道
NAKASENDOU
WOW, THIS ROAD INTERSECTS WITH THE NAKASENDOU?
NAKASENDOU
ONE OF THE ROADS CREATED DURING THE EDO PERIOD. RAN FROM EDO (NOW TOKYO) TO KYOTO.
EDO
KYOTO
中山道
NAKASENDOU
WHY ARE YOU MAKING THAT FACE?

WHOA.
WE MADE IT TO THE USUI HOT SPRING.
WELCOME, WEARY TRAVELERS.
WE SHOULD BE ABOUT A QUARTER OF THE WAY.
THAT WAS FAST.
HUH?
NADE-SHIKO-CHAN, ISN'T THIS A STATION?
YES.

THERE IS A STATION HERE AND THEN ONE AT THE MUSEUM.
SCENIC OLD-STYLE TRAINS USUALLY RUN ON THE WEEKENDS AND HOLIDAYS.
OOH.
IT'S LIKE THE LITTLE TRAINS YOU SEE AT AMUSEMENT PARKS.
BUT SINCE WE WALKED THE ABT ROAD TO GET HERE...
...WE'LL HAVE TO DO THE OLD-STYLE TRAIN ANOTHER TIME.
I WOULD ALSO LOVE TO STOP OFF AT THE USUI HOT SPRING AND SOAK MY EXHAUSTION AWAY...
...BUT IF WE STOP NOW, OUR PLANS WILL FALL TOTALLY APART.
ALAS!
SO THE USUI HOT SPRING MUST WAIT!!
NOT LIKE WE'RE ALL THAT TIRED TO BEGIN WITH.

OH HEY.
WHAT ABOUT YOUR SPECIAL IMAGI-NATION SKILL, EMA-CHAN?
MY WHAT?
EMA-CHAN HAS A SPECIAL GIFT. SHE CAN SUMMON IMAGINARY FRIENDS AT WILL.
SHE CAN?
SO ...
...WHY DON'T YOU SUMMON AN IMAGINARY HOT SPRING AND IMAGINE YOU GOT IN?
I HAVE NO IDEA WHAT ANY-THING AFTER "SO" MEANT.
SENPAI, WE'D BETTER NOT DAWDLE.
IT'LL EAT UP OUR TIME AT THE MUSEUM.
OH YEAH.
YOU'RE RIGHT. WE GOTTA HURRY.

BUT I NEVER CONSID-ERED DREAMING UP AN IMAGI-NARY HOT SPRING...
INTER-ESTING. I SHOULD TRY IT.
HOT SPRING.
HOT SPRING.
HOT SPRING.
HOT SPRING.
BUO (FWOOSH)
COME TO ME, HOT SPRING!!

EMA-CHAN, IS SOMETHING THE MATTER?
N-NO, NOTHING...
PUKUKU (PBBFFT)
PUPU

OH.
LOOKS LIKE SOME OF THE TRACKS ARE EX-POSED ON THIS STRETCH OF THE ROAD.
HERE IT ACTUALLY DOES FEEL LIKE WE'RE WALKING ON AN ABAN-DONED RAILWAY.
HELLO THERE.
HELLO.
WE'RE RUNNING INTO MORE PEOPLE NOW.
YEAH.

OLD-MARUYAMA SUBSTATION
A SUB-STATION BUILT DURING THE MEIJI ERA TO SUPPLY POWER TO ABT SYSTEM TRAINS TRAVELING THROUGH USUI PASS.
THIS BUILDING LOOKS LESS LIKE AN OLD SUB-STATION AND MORE LIKE A LIBRARY OR SCHOOL-HOUSE.
SENPAI, DO YOU SEE ANY-THING INSIDE?
SERI-OUSLY, WHAT IS WITH THAT FACE?

OH.
LOOK AT THAT, YOU TWO.
WASHA (GROOM)
わしゃ
わしゃ
WASHA
THERE ARE MON-KEYS ON TOP OF THE POWER POLE.
OH YEAH.
WOW, ALL THE WAY UP THERE?
すすす
SUSUSU (SIDLE)
S-SEN-PAI.
HOW CUTE. I WONDER IF IT'S A MOTHER AND HER BABY?
IT'S BETTER NOT TO GET TOO CLOSE TO WILD MONKEYS.

I'VE HEARD OF PEOPLE BEING ATTACKED FOR...
... STARTLING THEM OR LOOKING THEM IN THE EYES.
HSS AH!
Y-YEAH!?
I'VE HEARD YOU'RE NOT SUPPOSED TO LOCK EYES WITH WILD ANIMALS...
チラッ
CHIRA (GLANCE)
チラッ
CHIRA
BUT IF YOU TURN YOUR HEAD AWAY AND JUST GLANCE AT THEM, IS THAT OKAY?
I'M NO EXPERT, BUT IF YOU DRAW THEIR ATTENTION, IT COULD STILL BE A PROBLEM, RIGHT?
WHAT ABOUT IF I ROLL MY EYES BACK IN MY HEAD?
CAN I LOOK AT THEM LIKE THIS?
WHAT WOULD BE THE POINT?

HEY BOSS, IT LOOKS LIKE THEY'RE TOO HUNG UP ON GROOMING EACH OTHER TO NOTICE THE LIKES OF US ANYWAY.
WASHA (GROOM) わしゃ
WASHA わしゃ
SEEMS LIKE IT. HEH HEH HEH.
THEN LET'S MAKE OUR EXIT WHILE THEY'RE DISTRACTED.
SA (SHF) さ
さ SA
さ SA
さ SA
さ SA
さ SA
YIS-SIR.
THE WHOLE ROLLING-MY-EYES-BACK THING HAS GOT ME THINKING.
WHEN SOMEONE SAYS YOUR EYES "ROLL BACK IN YOUR HEAD," IT'S KINDA STRANGE, RIGHT?

IMAGINE IF WE TOOK THAT LITERALLY.
OHH, I SEE WHAT YOU MEAN.
"GIVING SOMEONE A FUNNY LOOK"...
... MEANS YOU'D END UP LIKE THIS.
THAT'S "MAKING A FUNNY FACE."
PYOKO (POP) ぴょこ
WHAT ABOUT DOGS GIVING WHALE EYES?
MYOOON (STREEETCH) みょーん
OR WHEN THEY SAY "TAKING A LONG-TERM VIEW"?
MEDIUM FATTY TUNA
HOW ABOUT DEAD FISH EYES?
THAT LOOKS LIKE SOMEONE WHO LOVES SUSHI A LITTLE TOO MUCH.

MAN, LANGUAGE IS TOUGH.
AH-HA-HA-HA-HA.
RIGHT?
MY SENPAI REALLY ARE WEIRD ...
YAAAAAAAAAAAAAAAAAAAAY!
SNAP
TO THINK WE'D SEE SOMETHING LIKE THAT ALL THE WAY OUT HERE.
SO WE HAD TO TAKE A PIC.
YEAH.
IT LOOKED LIKE A HIGHWAY.
OHH.

SIGN: ABT ROAD / / APUTO NO MITI

USUI CHECKPOINT
A CHECKPOINT ON THE NAKESENDOU ROAD BETWEEN MATSUIDA-SHUKU AND SAKAMOTO-SHUKU.
WE MADE IT!!!
WE AREN'T THERE YET.
AND SO, THEY REACHED THEIR REAL GOAL, THE STARTING POINT OF THE ABT ROAD.
WALKING TRAIL
ABT ROAD (START)
WE'RE HERE!!

AHH ...
WALKING THAT MUCH ON MY OWN LEGS MAKES ME FEEL SO ACCOM-PLISHED.
RIGHT?
IT WAS PRETTY FUN WALKING IT OUR-SELVES.
YAY!
CON-GRATS, EMA-CHAN!
GU (JAB)
UH, THANK YOU?
WHOA.
11:55
MAY 2ND (SAT)
WE MADE IT FIVE MINUTES AHEAD OF SCHED-ULE.
WE'RE ON A ROLL.

EMA-CHAN, ARE YOU TIRED?
NO.
IT WAS A DOWNHILL WALK.
I'M LESS TIRED THAN I EXPECTED.
I'M ALSO SURPRISED I'M NOT TIRED.
SO YOU'RE OKAY IF WE TAKE...
...A LOOK AROUND THE MUSEUM?
WE'RE LOW ON TIME, SO LET'S GO.
THAT'S WHY WE'RE HERE, AFTER ALL.
HOORAY!

BUOOOOO
(VRRRROM)
THE CAR WITH THE ROUND LIGHTS SHE WANTS TO DRIVE SOMEDAY

OH!
HULLO!
THE VINTAGE TRAINS ARE RIGHT UP FRONT!
OH MAN! THIS IS GREAT!
NADE-SHIKO-CHAN, WHAT KIND OF TRAIN IS THIS?
TRIVIA AND DETAILS ARE BEYOND ME!
WHAAAA?

CHAPTER 92
WELCOME TO THE YOKOKAWA RAIL MUSEUM

THESE TRAINS APPARENTLY CHECK THE TRACKS.
WOW.
DOESN'T THE ENTRANCE REMIND YOU OF MEGANE BRIDGE?
YEAH, IT DOES!

THERE ARE TONS OF FAMILIES WITH YOUNG KIDS.
IT IS GOLDEN WEEK.
AND KIDS LOVE RIDES, AFTER ALL.
CHILDHOOD EXPERIENCES MUST LEAD TO ADULT OBSESSIONS.
WHEEE!
I FEEL LIKE I'VE HEARD THAT SOMEWHERE BEFORE...
IN OTHER WORDS, THIS PLACE TURNS CHILDREN INTO TRAIN MANIACS.
YEEE!
IT'S LIKE SOME SORT OF SECRET BRAINWASHING FACILITY!!
YEEE!
EMA-CHAN, IS SOMETHING WRONG? YOU HAVE A SCARY LOOK ON YOUR FACE.
IT'S NOTHING.
?

YO!
THIS TRAIN IS IMPRESSIVE.
THE COLORING IS VERY MID-20TH CENTURY.
THIS TRAIN IS CUTE, KINDA LOOKS LIKE A BIRD.
A BIRD?
SEE? THAT PART LOOKS LIKE A BEAK AND THAT LOOKS LIKE WINGS.
HMM?
SARA (SCRBL)
サラ サラ
SARA
LIKE THIS?

CHEEP!
YEAH, THAT'S IT!
OHH, I SEE IT NOW.
OLD TRAINS ARE SO ANGULAR.
I LIKE HOW IT MAKES THEM LOOK LIKE ANIMALS.
LOOK! THAT ONE LOOKS LIKE A FUGU! HOW CUTE!
I AIN'T A FUGU!
FUGU... REALLY?
LIKE THIS?
PUKU (PUFF) プク
PUKU プク
OHH, NOW IT IS A FUGU.

MIMICRY
I SEE IT.
SNAP
IT IS KINDA FUN TO LOOK AT THIS LIKE A ZOO.
MM-HEH-HEH.

IS SOMETHING THE MATTER?
NO, IT'S JUST ...
IF THESE TRAINS WERE THE STARS OF A CHILDREN'S ANIME...
...THEN MAYBE AFTER THE MUSEUM CLOSED, THEY WOULD SNEAK OUT AND HAVE SOME FUN.
BUOOOO (HOOONK)
AHAAAA.
GOAAAAA (VRRRROOSH)
LIKE THIS?
EMA-CHAN, YOU'RE GOOD.

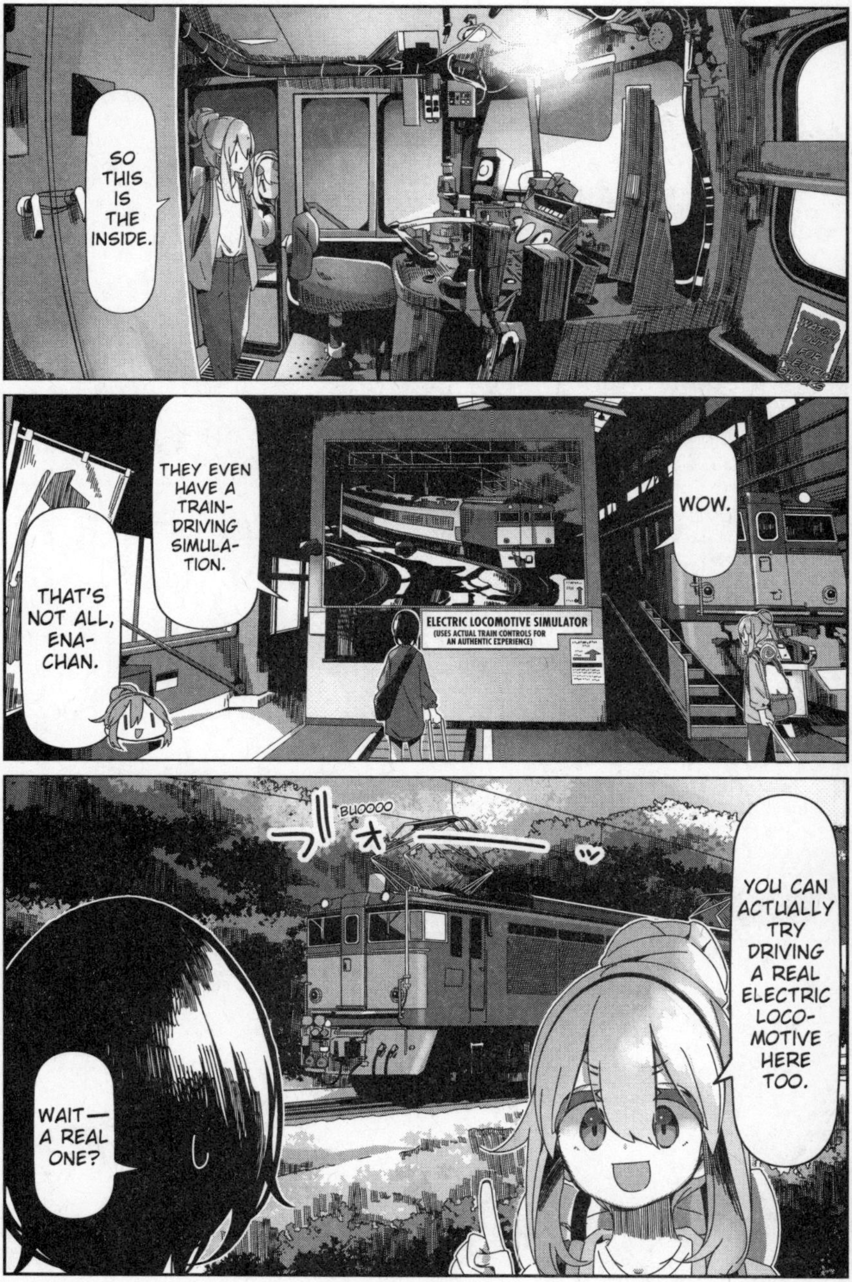
SO THIS IS THE INSIDE.
WATCH OUT FOR ELECTRIC SHOCKS
WOW.
THEY EVEN HAVE A TRAIN-DRIVING SIMULATION.
ELECTRIC LOCOMOTIVE SIMULATOR
(USES ACTUAL TRAIN CONTROLS FOR AN AUTHENTIC EXPERIENCE)
THAT'S NOT ALL, ENA-CHAN.
BUOOOO
YOU CAN ACTUALLY TRY DRIVING A REAL ELECTRIC LOCOMOTIVE HERE TOO.
WAIT— A REAL ONE?

THE PROCESS TO GET TO DRIVE A REAL ELECTRIC LOCOMOTIVE
FIRST IS TO SIGN UP FOR A TRAINING COURSE.
POCHI (CHK)
ポチッ
THEN TAKE THE ONE DAY TRAINING COURSE.
IF YOU CAN PASS THE FINAL EXAM...
SURE TO SUCCEED
...THEN YOU CAN SCHEDULE YOUR OWN DRIVING DEMO, FREE AND CLEAR.
SURE TO SUCCEED
YOU PASSED
UH, IS THIS A DRIVING SCHOOL?
IN THE BEGINNING, YOU CAN ONLY TAKE THE TRAIN OUT AND THEN BACK.
ELECTRIC LOCOMOTIVE APPRENTICE
DRIVE OVER 9 TIMES
ELECTRIC LOCOMOTIVE ASSISTANT
DRIVE OVER 29 TIMES
ELECTRIC LOCOMOTIVE REGULAR
DRIVE OVER 49 TIMES
ELECTRIC LOCOMOTIVE MASTER
DRIVE OVER 500 TIMES
AFTER TEST DRIVING OVER AND OVER, YOU CAN INCREASE YOUR RANK...
...AND YOU'LL BE ABLE TO HANDLE VARIOUS TYPES OF DRIVING.
ISN'T THAT JUST JOB TRAINING?
THAT COULD GET EXPENSIVE.
AND YOU SAID YOU HAVE TO DO IT A BUNCH...
THIS IS DEFINITELY AN ADULT HOBBY...
YOKOKAWA RAIL MUSEUM

-SNAP-
I HAD NO INTEREST IN TRAINS OR ANYTHING...
...BUT LOOKING INTO SOMETHING I KNOW NOTHING ABOUT IS STIMULATING—NOT SO BAD FROM TIME TO TIME.
THIS LOOKS STEAM-PUNK-ISH. IT'S REALLY COOL.

IT REALLY DOES LOOK LIKE A FUGU.
HERE IT IS!
COMMEMORATIVE DOMESTIC ABT SYSTEM RAILWAY
OCTOBER 14TH, SHOWA 42 (1967)
OOH.

THIS IS THE ONE I WANTED TO SEE MOST.
THIS IS AN ACTUAL ABT CAR THAT USED TO RUN ALONG THE ABT ROAD.
I SEE.
HAVE A LOOK UNDER HERE.

THESE COGS WOULD LATCH ONTO THE LITTLE NODULES EMBEDDED INTO THE GROUND.
SINCE THEY HAD TO GO UP SUCH STEEP HILLS.
HEY!
SO THAT'S WHAT'S UNDER-NEATH!
YOU SURE KNOW A LOT ABOUT ABT TRAINS.
HEH HEH HEH.
THEY HAD AN ABT LOCO-MOTIVE AT OIGAWA TOO.
OIGAWA?
RIDING THAT GOT ME INTER-ESTED IN OLDER TRAINS.
LET'S SEE...
HERE IT IS.

I RODE THIS RED ABT TRAIN INTO THE DEEP PARTS OF OIGAWA—THE AREA AROUND THE OOI RIVER.
6
WE RODE UPHILL ALONG THE OOI RIVER THE WHOLE WAY.
LIKE HERE.
A DAM?
AND WE WENT TO PLACES LIKE THIS.
OH, I'VE SEEN PIC-TURES OF THIS PLACE BEFORE.

THIS LOOKS LIKE IT WAS FUN.
IT WAS A LOT OF FUN.
AND I GOT PICS OF THE KASH-ING.
?
THE KASH-ING?
THE ABT TRAINS IN OIGAWA ALSO HAD LIGHTS AND WINDOWS THAT LOOKED LIKE FACES, WHICH MADE THEM KINDA CUTE.
YO!
LONG TIME, NO SEE!
THEY ALL LOOK LIKE FISH.
THIS ABT TRAIN ...
...IS BROWN WITH JUST ONE LIGHT, SO IT LOOKS LIKE A FATTENED MONK-FISH.

LIKE THIS?
AH-HA-HA. THAT IS SO GOOD.
ブク
BUKU
ブク
BUKU (INFLATE)
OH, WHERE DID ENA-CHAN GO?
HUH?
OVER HERE.
DID SOMETHING HAPPEN?
YEAH.
IT LOOKS LIKE YOU CAN CAMP AT THIS MUSEUM.
OH, YOU CAN?

YOKOKAWA RAIL MUSEUM AUTOCAMP
AN OUTDOOR EXPERIENCE YOU CAN ONLY HAVE HERE, SURROUNDED BY TRAINS FROM DAYS GONE BY.
DATES
29 4/30
WE TAKE APPLICATIONS VIA X
ACCEPTING THE FIRST 23 PARTIES FOR
SEE— THEY DO IT FROM TIME TO TIME AS AN EVENT.
WOW, I HAD NO IDEA THEY HAD SOME-THING LIKE THIS.
AND IT LOOKS LIKE THEY JUST HELD ONE LAST NIGHT...
AWW, LAST NIGHT!?
DATES
4/29 4/30 5/1
WE TAKE APPLICATIONS VIA XXXXXX
(ACCEPTING THE FIRST 23 PARTIES FOR EACH DATE)
WHOA, YOU'RE RIGHT...
IF WE HAD KNOWN SOONER, WE COULD HAVE CAMPED HERE.
SO I COULDA CAMPED OUTSIDE, SUR-ROUNDED BY TRAINS?
I WISH I HAD DONE A LITTLE MORE RESEARCH...

ALL RIGHT!
THE NEXT TIME I COME, I'M CAMPING HERE!!
ば
BA (BOM)
THEN I CAN WALK THE ABT ROAD FROM KUMANO-TAIRA.
EAT AT CLUB-MAN.
GET IN THE HOT SPRING AND RIDE THE RAILCARS!
YOU SHOULD DO IT.
I WANT TO GO BACK TO CLUBMAN.

KASHA (SNAP)
カシャ

鉄道資料館
-BEE- -BEE- -BEE- -BEE- -BEEP-
-BEE- -BEE- -BEE- -BEE- -BEEP-
HM?
ALARM 12:50
OH!
PERFECT TIMING.

WE DID A LAP AROUND THE MUSEUM, BUT IT DIDN'T TAKE THAT LONG.
WELL, I JUST LIKE THE TRAINS. I'M NO AFICIO-NADO.
IF I WERE SOME-ONE WHO KNEW ALL ABOUT EACH AND EVERY TRAIN...
...IT COULD TAKE ME ALL DAY.
GOOD POINT.
I'M SORRY FOR MAKING YOU TWO GO SOME-WHERE ONLY I WAS INTO.
NOT AT ALL.
I'M GLAD I GOT TO SEE THE VINTAGE TRAINS TOO.

AND I FEEL A SORT OF AFFINITY FOR THEM WALKING THESE ABAN-DONED TRACKS.
YEAH, I GET THAT.
OH, GOOD.
WE'VE BEEN RUSHING JUST TO MAKE IT ALL DAY.
BUT ALL THAT'S LEFT IS TO GO SHOPPING AND HEAD TO THE CAMPSITE.
LET'S TAKE OUR TIME.
YEAH.
OKAY.
RIGHT BY YOKOKAWA STATION STOOD...
...THE MAIN PURVEYOR OF YOKOKAWA'S FAMOUS KAMAMESHI.

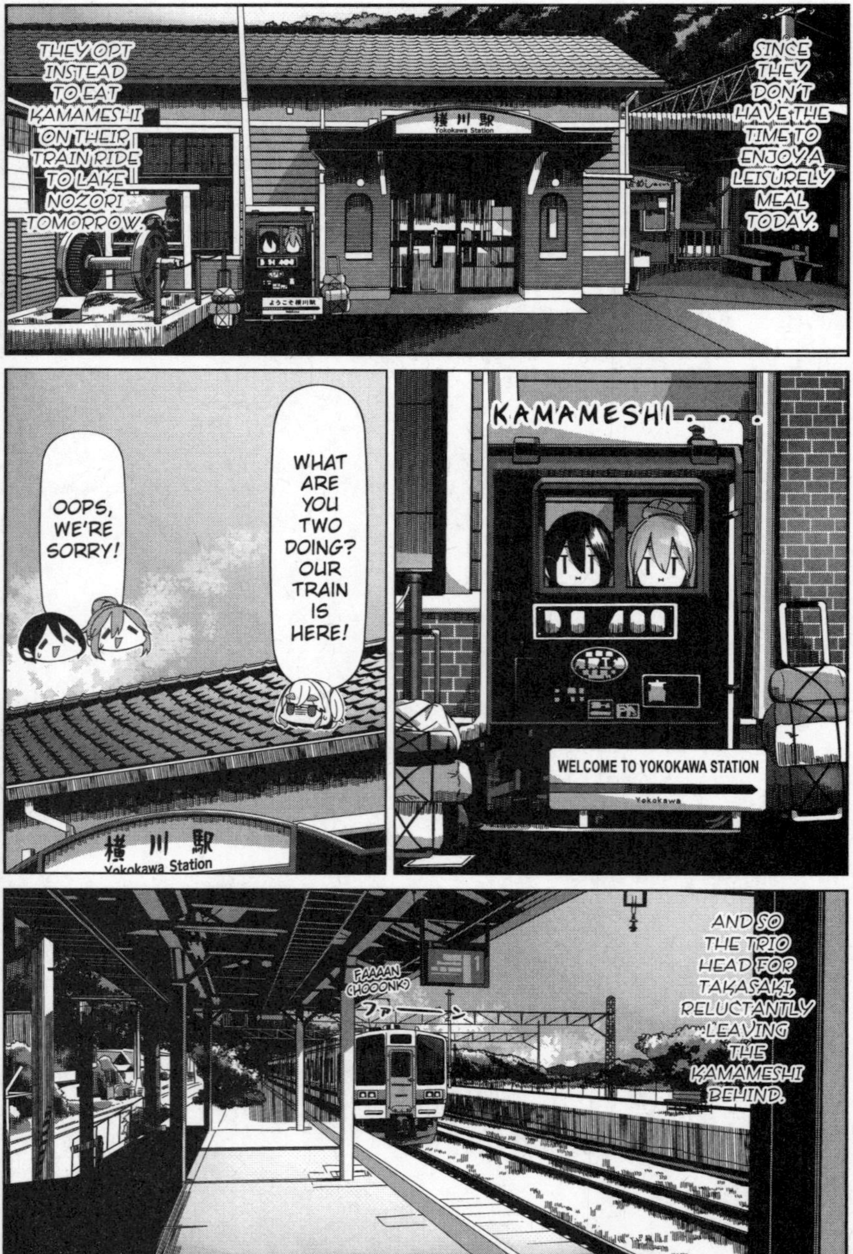
SINCE THEY DON'T HAVE THE TIME TO ENJOY A LEISURELY MEAL TODAY.
THEY OPT INSTEAD TO EAT KAMAMESHI ON THEIR TRAIN RIDE TO LAKE NOZORI TOMORROW.
横川駅
Yokokawa Station
KAMAMESHI . . .
WELCOME TO YOKOKAWA STATION
Yokokawa
WHAT ARE YOU TWO DOING? OUR TRAIN IS HERE!
OOPS, WE'RE SORRY!
横 川 駅
Yokokawa Station
AND SO THE TRIO HEAD FOR TAKASAKI, RELUCTANTLY LEAVING THE KAMAMESHI BEHIND.
FAAAAN (HOOONK)
ファーーン

TRANSLATION NOTES

COMMON HONORIFICS
no honorific: Indicates familiarity or closeness; if used without permission or reason, addressing someone in this manner would constitute an insult.
-san: The Japanese equivalent of Mr./Mrs./Miss. If a situation calls for politeness, this is the fail-safe honorific.
-kun: Used most often when referring to boys, this indicates affection or familiarity. Occasionally used by older men among their peers, but it may also be used by anyone referring to a person of lower standing.
-chan: An affectionate honorific indicating familiarity used mostly in reference to girls; also used in reference to cute persons or animals regardless of gender.
-sensei: A respectful term for teachers, artists, or high-level professionals.

(o)nee: Japanese equivalent to "older sis."
(o)nii: Japanese equivalent to "older bro."

100 yen is usually approximately 1 USD, though the exact amount can fluctuate greatly. As of 2024, it is about 65 cents USD.
1 centimeter is approximately 0.39 inches. 1 kilometer is approximately 0.621 miles.

PAGE 3
Golden Week: A holiday season in Japan that runs from late April to early May and consists of four holidays: Showa Day, Constitution Day, Greenery Day, and Children's Day. A great many people usually have off during this time, so it's popular for vacation and travel.

PAGE 4
Yokokawa Rail Museum: Based on the real-life Usui Pass Railway Heritage Park found between Yokokawa, Gunma and Karuizawa, Nagano.

PAGE 6
Nebuta Festival: Also known as the Aomori Nebuta Festival, this is one of the three major festivals in the Tohoku region of Japan. It is known for its large and elaborate floats, which Ena's styling of Rin's hair emulates.

PAGE 19
Waraji katsu: Short for *waraji katsudon*, this is an extra-large dish consisting of a pork cutlet in a rice bowl and served with a sweet and salty sauce. Its cutlets resemble straw sandals called *waraji*.

Irago *kaisendon*: Irago is a cape located in Aichi Prefecture. *Kaisendon* is literally "seafood bowl" and is a dish of sashimi served over plain white rice (as opposed to vinegared sushi rice).

Food porn: In Japanese, the equivalent term is *meshi tero*, or "food terrorism."

TRANSLATION NOTES (continued)

PAGE 34
Kamameshi: A dish of rice, meats, and vegetables cooked together in an iron pot. Originally, the iron pot was a communal dish meant to feed people after the Great Kanto Earthquake of 1923. The *kamameshi* sold by Yokokawa Station is a famous *ekiben* (train station lunch) that even comes in a unique container.

PAGE 61
Anko: A sweetened red-bean paste made from *azuki* beans typically used as a filling for snacks and desserts.
Monaka: A Japanese dessert snack consisting of two wafer shells around a filling.

PAGES 97–100
Eye-based idioms: Many of the idioms here have been changed from the original Japanese.
***Shiroi me de miru* ("look with white eyes")**: Stare coldly
***Hen na me de miru* ("look with strange eyes")**: Give a funny look
***Hengao* ("strange face")**: Make a funny face
***Mekujira tateru* ("eye whales are standing")**: Find fault over minor quibbles

PAGE 112
Fugu: A Japanese blowfish that is considered a delicacy despite possessing an extremely powerful and often deadly toxin.

PAGE 122
Kashing: Originally "buppigan," this is an onomatopoeia of a clanging sound commonly heard in anime, especially the Gundam franchise.

PAGE 133
Minami-Alps: Literally "Southern Alps," this is the name of a city in Yamanashi Prefecture.

PAGE 159
Tsukapon: A fictional mascot and snack that appears in the theatrical film *Laid-Back Camp Movie*.

Saury, not amberjack: This is a reference to the fact that the written character for amberjack fish (鰍) is often misread as *sanma* instead of the correct *kajika*. This is partly because pacific saury (i.e., *sanma*) look very similar to amberjack, and therefore the two are hard to tell apart.

SPECIAL EPISODE RIN AND NADESHIKO'S LAKE INAGA SPRING CAMP

MADE IT TO LAKE INAGA.
HMMM.
THE FOREST SITES ARE ON THE OTHER SIDE OF THIS PARKING LOT.
THE LAKE-SIDE SITES ARE ON THE OTHER SIDE OF THE REST HOUSE.

TODAY'S LUNCH SPECIAL
FOREST SOUP CURRY
WITH LONG SPICY SAUSAGE!!
¥1,000
FOREST SOUP CURRY ...
GOKURI (GULP)
ゴクリ
FIRST I NEED TO HEAD TO RECEPTION.
THE ADMINISTRATIVE BUILDING ...
... LOOKS LIKE IT'S OVER HERE.

THIS IS NOT THE ADMINISTRATIVE BUILDING.
LOOKS LIKE IT'S OVER THERE.
ADMINISTRATIVE BUILDING
ADMINISTRATIVE BUILDING
ADMINISTRATIVE BUILDING

HELLO, MAY I PLEASE RESERVE ONE LAKESHORE SITE FOR ONE NIGHT?
AND MAY I GET A BUNDLE OF FIREWOOD, PLEASE?
PLEASE FILL IN YOUR NAME AND ADDRESS HERE.
SEVERAL DAYS EARLIER
RIN-CHAN!
I FOUND A MYSTERIOUS CAMPSITE IN THE MINAMI-ALPS MOUNTAINS!
A MYSTERIOUS CAMPSITE?
Yeah!
I found it looking around on Goggle Maps.
It's a lakeshore campsite—the kind you like...
...and it even has a scenic overlook where you can look out over Koufu.

OH, THAT'S INA-GAKO.
You've heard of it, Rin-chan?
I'VE PASSED IT ON THE ROAD MANY TIMES, AND KNEW ABOUT THE LAKE AS WELL.
But I can't be-lieve they have a camp-site.
WOW.
WE HAVE A LITTLE SPRING BREAK LEFT, SO HOW ABOUT ONE LAST CAMPING TRIP?
All right. I'm in.
BZZT
BZZT
10:05
Made it to Kajikazawa! (>0<)
10:05
Now heading up to the campsite on my bike!

FROM KAJIKA-ZAWA WOULD BE ABOUT 10 KM.
KNOWING NADE-SHIKO'S STAMINA, SHE'LL PROBA-BLY GET HERE JUST BEFORE NOON.
HUFF...
HUFF...
HUFF...
WHEEEEW!

HMMM.
MT. FUJI'S A BIT FOGGY RIGHT NOW, SO I CAN'T REALLY SEE IT.
OKAY.
JUST A LITTLE FARTHER TO LAKE INAGA!
EVERYTHING'S ALL SET.

HERE THE GRASSY AREAS AND CAMPING SPACES ARE CLEARLY SEPARATED.
IT'S A LITTLE PRICEY, BUT WE'RE NOT PACKED IN LIKE AT THE OPEN CAMPSITES.
THIS PLACE IS NICE AND FEELS MORE SPACIOUS.

THAT'S A GIANT FISH.

GISHI
(CREAK)
ギシ
......
I GUESS THIS PLACE REALLY IS A HIDDEN GEM, HUH?

-BZZZT-
-BZZZT-
A HOT SPRING, EH?
11:10
I found a hot spring in the mountains!!
HM?
DID I SEE ANY HOT SPRINGS ON MY WAY HERE?
SHAAAA (SWSSSSH)
シャーーーッ

SHAAAAA (SWSSSSH)
WHOOOOOOOOOOA!!
SHAAAAA
OOOOOOOOOOOOAH!!
SHAAAAA

OH?
I KNOW IT'S S'POSED TO BE A STRAIGHT SHOT TO THE CAMP-SITE!
SHAAAAA
シャー
WHOOOOOOOA!!
SHAAAAA
シャーーッ
!!
BUT IS IT SUP-POSED TO BE THIS FAST—??
シャーッ
SHAAAAA

WHOOOA!
YOU MADE IT!
THE TAKAORI DIAMOND FUJI SUNRISE ...
AHA!!
IS THAT WHERE AKI-CHAN AND THE OTHERS WENT FOR NEW YEAR'S?

WHAT IS THIS PLACE? YOU CAN SEE MT. FUJI SO WELL...
IS IT A PARKING LOT?
I SEE.
SO THIS IS THE DIAMOND FUJI SPOT.
......HUH?
SO DOES THAT MEAN ...

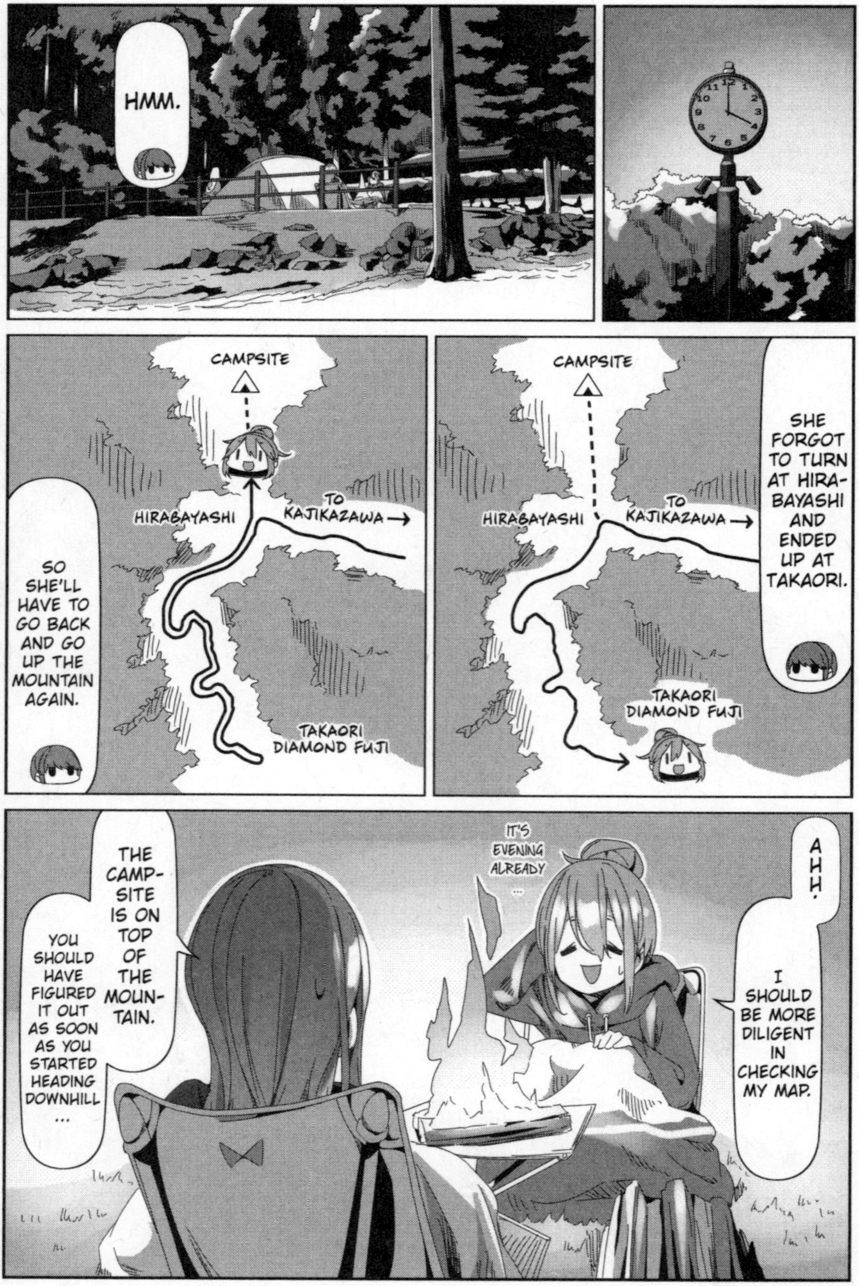
HMM.
CAMPSITE
HIRABAYASHI
TO KAJIKAZAWA →
TAKAORI DIAMOND FUJI
SHE FORGOT TO TURN AT HIRA-BAYASHI AND ENDED UP AT TAKAORI.
CAMPSITE
HIRABAYASHI
TO KAJIKAZAWA →
TAKAORI DIAMOND FUJI
SO SHE'LL HAVE TO GO BACK AND GO UP THE MOUNTAIN AGAIN.
AHH.
IT'S EVENING ALREADY ...
I SHOULD BE MORE DILIGENT IN CHECKING MY MAP.
THE CAMP-SITE IS ON TOP OF THE MOUN-TAIN.
YOU SHOULD HAVE FIGURED IT OUT AS SOON AS YOU STARTED HEADING DOWNHILL ...

JUUUU (SIZZZZLE)
ジウー
PACHI (KRAKL)
パチッ
PACHI
パチ
PETA (SMEAR)
ぺた
PETA
ぺた
PACHI
パチ
IS IT READY YET?
パチッ
PACHI

THERE.
AND NOW JUST TO SPRINKLE ON SOME CINNAMON...
ビィーン
BIIIN (VRRRRREEN)
NADESHIKO, I GOT THE ICE CREAM.
THANK YOU, RIN-CHAN.
I MADE IT JUST BEFORE THE REST HOUSE CLOSED UP.
GOOD THING.
LAST BUT NOT LEAST, TOP IT WITH ICE CREAM ...

パ—ン!
BAAAAN (DUDUUUUN)
ALL DONE !!
I THINK THAT'S WAY TOO MUCH ICE CREAM.
ROASTED APPLE DESSERT TORTILLAS
BON APPÉ-HIH.
MGLP-GLP.
SEE— IT IS TOO MUCH ICE CREAM. IT'S TOO DIFFICULT TO EAT.
MGLP-GLP.
GLP GLP.
THAT WAS GOOD.
SHO GOOD.

THE CHICKEN TORTILLA I ATE BEFORE WAS GOOD, BUT MAKING A SWEET VERSION CAME OUT WELL TOO.
RIGHT?
I THOUGHT A TORTILLA WOULD BE A GOOD FIT FOR CAMPING.
JUST THE FACT THAT YOU PUT THE INGREDIENTS IN IT MEANS LESS DISHES TO WASH.
MM-HM.
WHEN WE DO ANOTHER COOKING CAMP, WE SHOULD MAKE A BUNCH OF DIFFERENT STUFF, THEN WRAP IT IN ONE OF THESE TO EAT IT.
OH, GOOD IDEA.
THIS REALLY IS GOOD.
OM NOM.
IT'S ALSO GOOD IF YOU SPREAD CREAM CHEESE ON IT, ADD KIWI, AND TOP IT WITH MANGO SAUCE AND WHIPPED CREAM.
OOH.

HMM... I GUESS THERE ISN'T ANY NEARBY.
WHAT'S UP?
WELL.
I WAS LOOKING TO SEE IF THERE WERE ANY CAMP-SITES NEAR TAKAORI, BUT THERE AREN'T ANY.
I WAS THINKING IF THERE WERE CAMP-SITES AT TAKAORI ...
...IT WOULD BE NICE FOR US TO BE ABLE TO SEE DIAMOND FUJI FOR NEW YEAR'S CAMP.
OH YEAH.
THERE ARE SO MANY NEW CAMP-SITES BEING BUILT BECAUSE OF THE CAMPING BOOM.
I HOPE THEY BUILD ONE THERE.
YEAH.
IF THEY BUILT A CAMPSITE THERE, THE VIEW WOULD BE SO GOOD THAT IT WOULD BECOME A POPULAR CAMPING SPOT.
IT'D BE A REAL SCRAM-BLE TO GET A RESER-VATION FOR NEW YEAR'S EVE.
ESPECIALLY FOR PEOPLE WANTING TO SEE DIAMOND FUJI.
AH-HA-HA. YOU'RE RIGHT.

IF THEY BUILD A CAMP-SITE, I HOPE IT'S A GRASSY ONE.
I WOULD LIKE A QUIET PLACE WHERE I COULD CAMP IN PRIVATE.
AND I DON'T NEED ANY SHOPS, BUT I WOULD WANT THEM TO HAVE FIRE-WOOD FOR SALE.
ME TOO.
AND A PLACE THAT ALLOWS PETS SO DOGS CAN STAY OVER WOULD BE GOOD.
THEN CHI-KUWA COULD COME WITH US.
RIN-CHAN! LET'S COME SEE DIAMOND FUJI NEXT YEAR!
SURE... IF I REMEM-BER.

AFTER-SCHOOL 126 LET'S TRY HANGING A HAMMOCK IN THE CLUBROOM

LET'S SEE. FIRST, WE NEED TO SEEK OUT A STUD TO STABILIZE THE HAMMOCK WITH THIS SENSOR.
WOW, SO THEY MAKE MACHINES LIKE THAT TO USE?
A SENSOR FOR DETECTING STUDS AND JOISTS IN THE WALLS.
OOH!
THIS BEAM LOOKS STURDY ENOUGH.
ピーピーピー
PI (BEE) PI PI
WHA—?
パカッ
PAKA (POP)

AFTER-SCHOOL 127 LET'S TRY HANGING A HAMMOCK IN THE CLUBROOM OTHERWORLD EDITION

BATAN (SLAM)
バタン
GAN (BANG)
ガン
GAN
ガン
GAN
ガン
WE DID IT—!!
OUR CLUB HAM-MOCK IS DONE!!

HOW DID YOU LIKE VOLUME 16 OF *LAID-BACK CAMP*?
THIS VOLUME CONTAINS THE TRIALS OF RIN'S HAIR AND THE FIRST HALF OF THE GUNMA CAMPING TRIP.
THE ABT ROAD THAT APPEARS IN CHAPTERS 90-91 REALLY FEELS LIKE A FANTASY DUNGEON, COMPLETE WITH AN OTHERWORLDLY TUNNEL AND WILDLIFE THAT JUST SUDDENLY APPEARS OUT OF NOWHERE. EVEN IF YOU'RE NOT INTO TRAINS, I RECOMMEND A VISIT.

THIS HAS BEEN AFRO.

[PUBLICATION LIST]
• *COMIC FUZ* APRIL AND JUNE 2021, JULY–DECEMBER 2023
• *LAID-BACK CAMP MOVIE* SPECIAL BONUS EXTRA FOR THEATERGOERS: "*LAID-BACK CAMP VOLUME 13.5*"
• NEW EXTRAS
THE MATERIALS IN THIS VOLUME WERE COLLECTED FROM THE ABOVE SOURCES.

LAID BACK CAMP 16

Afro

Translation: **Amber Tamosaitis** ❋ Lettering: **DK**

YURUCAMP Vol. 16

Yen Press
150 West 30th Street, 6th Floor
New York, NY 10001

Visit us at yenpress.com
facebook.com/yenpress
twitter.com/yenpress
yenpress.tumblr.com
instagram.com/yenpress

First Yen Press Edition: February 2025
Edited by Yen Press Editorial: Carl Li
Designed by Yen Press Design: Andy Swist, Wendy Chan

Yen Press is an imprint of Yen Press, LLC.
The Yen Press name and logo are trademarks of Yen Press, LLC.

The publisher is not responsible for websites (or their content) that are not owned by the publisher.

Library of Congress Control Number: 2017959206

ISBNs: 979-8-8554-0997-0 (paperback)
979-8-8554-0998-7 (ebook)

10 9 8 7 6 5 4 3 2 1

WOR

Printed in the United States of America